T0147399

And Justice For All

Girad Clacy

iUniverse, Inc.
New York   Bloomington

And Justice For All

Copyright © 2009 by Girad Clacy

All rights reserved. No part of this book may be used or reproduced by any means, graphic, electronic, or mechanical, including photocopying, recording, taping or by any information storage retrieval system without the written permission of the publisher except in the case of brief quotations embodied in critical articles and reviews.

This is a work of fiction. All of the characters, names, incidents, organizations, and dialogue in this novel are either the products of the author's imagination or are used fictitiously.

iUniverse books may be ordered through booksellers or by contacting:

iUniverse
1663 Liberty Drive
Bloomington, IN 47403
www.iuniverse.com
1-800-Authors (1-800-288-4677)

Because of the dynamic nature of the Internet, any Web addresses or links contained in this book may have changed since publication and may no longer be valid. The views expressed in this work are solely those of the author and do not necessarily reflect the views of the publisher, and the publisher hereby disclaims any responsibility for them.

ISBN: 978-1-4401-2252-1 (sc)
ISBN: 978-1-4401-2253-8 (ebk)

Printed in the United States of America

iUniverse rev. date: 02/16/2009

CHAPTER 1

A warm breeze blew gently down the open sidewalks around STARCORE headquarters and the various administration buildings. The sunlight was reflecting off the enormous skyscrapers as people walked in and out of the buildings. Anti-gravity cars passed overhead and unmanned taxicabs were picking up and dropping off passengers. One taxicab stopped in front of the STARCORE Legal Administration building and a lone figure stepped out of the unmanned vehicle. He then reached into the seat next to him and took out several bags of clothes. The taxicab said thank you to the passenger getting out and went about going to another call.

The figure walked up the white, marble stairs to the top and walked in through the open double-glass doors. Once he had stepped through the doorway, the doors silently shut behind him. He looked down at his own reflection in the black, alabaster floor.

The floor was etched with gold inlays that made the shape of a large woman, blindfolded and holding the balanced scales. Yes, Lady Justice was present. Directly underneath her were the words, "Truth and Justice For All People, All Races, Everywhere in the Galaxy."

The figure could see his reflection in the floor for one last time. The long, blond hair almost completely covered his uniform. He took in a long, deep breath and continued walking towards the elevators. He stepped into one of the available elevators and the doors closed behind him. Once the elevator was in motion, he reached into his top, left, uniform jacket pocket for the small, black disc that contained his STARCORE personnel record. As the elevator stopped on the 110th floor of the building, the figure straightened up.

He stepped out of the elevator and the doors closed behind him. He walked down the long hallway to the office at the end of the hallway. He knocked on the door and the door automatically opened for him. He stepped through and placed his STARCORE Personnel file into the hands of the secretary that was seated at the desk. He didn't say anything to her and immediately took a seat to the left of her desk. A few minutes later the door opened just behind and to the right of the secretary. A large man stepped out into the room and simply motioned for him to step into the office.

He stepped into the office and waited for the door to close. Once the door was closed, the large man looked at his STARCORE Personnel File. After a quick review, the large man stood back up again and looked at the man standing in front of him. The large man knew that this person was actually something that science referred to as a cyborg. During the man's last mission during the Great War with the Gardenians, he was severely hurt by an explosion. Several large pieces of computer equipment were blasted into the man's back, arms and legs.

STARCORE medical technology did the rest. The STARCORE medical files listed the man as STARCORE's only cyborg. The man was smart and was listed as FIT FOR DUTY according to the STARCORE medical officer who completed the man's medical exam only a few weeks before. The large man, Vice Admiral Harry Strauss, Commander STARCORE Legal Corps Academy, handed the small disc back to the man.

"What is your name?" asked Vice Admiral Strauss.

"Mike Weatherspoon, sir," the man replied.

"What is your rank?"

"Chief Warrant Officer Number One, sir."

"Are you human?"

"No, sir. I am a cyborg. I am the best of both worlds."

"What kind of training do you have?"

"I completed the eight year STARCORE Legal Corps Academy at the beginning of this year. I took the oral and written exams and scored very high on both. With a Fit For Duty clearance from STARCORE medical, I am now requesting to go aboard a STARCORE ship," replied Mike, confidently.

"Do you know why we here at STARCORE have kept you from going aboard a STARCORE vessel of any kind?"

"Yes, sir. It is because of my long, blond hair that is used to cover the surgical procedures done so that I may live."

"That's not the real reason."

"I know of one other. It is because I am not human and not machine, but a blending of the two. I could cause problems within not only the ranks of STARCORE, but my intelligence would let me outthink and outperform any commanding officer of any vessel that I am assigned."

"That is correct. Some would feel that you are a threat; why should I allow you to go aboard a STARCORE vessel to cause that much discontent?"

"I have learned how to be the best legal defense or prosecution person that I can be within my limits. By choosing the STARCORE Legal Corps, I have removed myself from any type of possibility of taking over command with my superior reflexes and intelligence, sir."

"Do you wish to add anything?"

"Yes, sir. In accordance with STARCORE Instruction 1611.112D, Paragraph 2, Subsection 3 states that once an injured STARCORE member is declared Fit For Duty, then that person shall be reassigned to a STARCORE ship as soon as possible, sir."

"Very well, I will consider your request on such grounds. Is there anything else?"

"Yes, sir. If you assign me to a STARCORE vessel, I respectfully request the USS PERFORMANCE, NCX-2105."

"Why that ship?" asked the vice admiral, raising his eyebrows a little.

"Several reasons. That ship has a need of a Legal Officer, which I do fill that qualification by STARCORE Instruction 111.99D, Paragraph 18, Subsection 12 and I happen to know someone aboard the ship."

"Wouldn't that be a conflict of interest?"

"No, sir. It becomes a conflict of interest if any or all of the following grounds are met in accordance with STARCORE Legal Instruction 113.11C. Since this person will not be in my chain of command, this relationship I have with this person will not violate the parameters of the STARCORE Legal Instruction."

"I will certainly give your request consideration."

"If you elect not to assign me to a STARCORE vessel, sir, then my time and effort was a waste of time on my part and the part of STARCORE. This waste of time on both parties parts would also constitute Fraud, Waste and Abuse of manpower and material in accordance with STARCORE protocols."

"Return to your holding cell, I will consider your request. I do have a few days to consider your request, don't I?"

"Yes, sir. You have 96 hours to either honor my request or else accept this," said Mike, handing the vice admiral another disc.

The vice admiral put the disc into the viewer and read the contents. The contents were all filed in accordance with STARCORE instructions. Mike's Letter of Resignation was complete and not missing anything. The vice admiral looked back up at Mike as he turned to walk out the door to return to his holding cell. As the door shut, Mike's thoughts turned to retirement and maybe moving to another planet where it wouldn't matter if he was human or machine or both. All he was looking for was acceptance.

Mike returned to his holding cell and ate dinner in the small cafeteria. Under constant escort by armed guards, more to prevent someone from kidnapping him than anything else, he walked around the small holding cell's grassy area. The small holding cell's 10-meter tall reinforced concrete walls would keep Mike from escaping.

He looked up at the setting sun and noticed how orange the sky turned at dusk. He took a shower and opened the small drawer on the nightstand next to his bed. He pulled out the picture frame, which contained the picture of himself and his lover. Mike vowed that he would get aboard the USS PERFORMANCE so he could be with his lover. Mike put the picture back into the drawer and went to sleep after turning off the light.

Meanwhile, aboard the USS PERFORMANCE, Captain Powers was looking over the ship's shakedown cruise. There were only a few things that were in need of adjustment and only one system that needed complete replacement. As he scanned over the list of crewmembers missing from the ship's compliment, he noticed that he needed another Legal Officer.

After setting the list down on the tabletop in his underway cabin, Captain Powers turned on his computer terminal that was sitting on the desktop. After he had turned the computer terminal on, the face of the communications officer appeared on the screen.

"Yes, sir, what can I do for you?" she asked.

"Please put me on live transmission link to STARCORE Fleet Headquarters Admiral Fantong," said Captain Powers.

"Yes, sir. Might I remind the captain that we are several thousand light years out from Earth and transmissions do take longer since I have to go through the transmitters aboard the space dock."

"I understand and I will wait."

"Yes, sir,"

In a few minutes, the image of STARCORE's Fleet Admiral, Admiral Fantong, appeared on the computer terminal screen. The admiral smiled as he saw whom it was trying to get in touch with him. Captain Powers looked at the screen and smiled.

"Good evening, Admiral Fantong, it is good to talk to you, sir," said Captain Powers.

"John, how are you doing?" replied the admiral, trying to keep another person in the room from knowing with whom he was talking.

"Fine, admiral, sir. I do have some personnel issues that I need to discuss with you. If this is not a good time to discuss this issue, then please let me know."

"This is a perfect time, John. What can I do for you?"

"I need a Legal Officer, sir. It appears that my legal assistant first class and the legal assistant third class cannot sign the paperwork necessary for all the legal issues aboard my ship."

"I hear you, John. At the present time, do you have any pressing legal issues?"

"Yes, sir. I have a member of my crew who was arrested and charged with First Degree Murder."

"Is that the crewmember who was involved with the USS SEA TIGER incident?"

"Yes, sir. That crewmember is currently in the ship's brig and is approaching the time when STARCORE must either formally charge the person or release him."

"I understand. Say, John, would you be interested in a little experiment that STARCORE is putting together?" asked the admiral, as he shifted his eyes from John to Vice Admiral Strauss.

"Sure, I would be interested in any order to participate in a STARCORE exercise."

"This STARCORE exercise as you call it, is not an order. If you accept this STARCORE exercise, it will be by your own choice. If you're interested, please go to secure transmissions."

John pushed a few buttons on the side of the computer terminal and the transmission was now considered secure. The ship's communications system began to immediately rotate the frequency and the modulation of the outgoing transmission; while at the same time, using the current 384 bit encryption coding, the outgoing transmission was scrambled. The incoming transmission was scrambled, had to be decoded and deencrypted so that it could be viewed and heard by the intended parties only.

"We're secure, admiral," said John.

"Okay. I have a very bright, young and energetic chief warrant officer that just finished off STARCORE Legal Corps Academy and specifically requested your ship as his first duty assignment."

"This chief warrant officer requested my ship, you say? Is he qualified?"

"Yes, however there is something about his past that your crew may not ever get used to about him."

"What's that?"

"He's a cyborg, John and his lover, as I understand, is aboard your ship."

"A cyborg? Is his lover in the same department?"

"No, his lover is in the weapons department, as I understand."

"I see. Admiral, it would be an honor to have him aboard my ship."

"I'll send him out to you within the next 48 hours. I will also be sending special orders ahead of him and could you please look the other way on his hair style."

"What's wrong with his hair?"

"The length of his hair covers the computer parts that run his body."

"Oh, I see. I will overlook that issue, sir."

"Thank you, John. Anything else I can do for you?"

"No admiral, I think we have taken care of it all. When will my first mission begin?"

"After your new legal officer arrives aboard, you will have your orders."

"Good night, sir."

"Good night, John,"

The transmissions terminated and both parties were allowed to think about what was going to happen. John, on his ship, sat back into his chair for a little while before retiring to his main cabin. As he sat back against his bed pillows that he had propped up earlier that afternoon, he started to put together a speech for the officers of the ship as to how to treat the new officer. He went to sleep still not finding the right words to say what he needed to say.

Meanwhile, back on Earth, Admiral Fantong looked up at Vice Admiral Strauss. He looked back down at the tabletop before he started typing up Mike's orders and the orders for the USS PERFORMANCE. As he completed typing the orders for Mike, he gave the orders to Vice Admiral Strauss.

"Are you happy, Vice Admiral Strauss?" asked Admiral Fantong.

"Quite happy, sir. I will inform Chief Warrant Officer Number One, Mike Weatherspoon, to be in uniform and ready for departure within the next 24 hours."

"Do you know why I assigned Mike to the USS PERFOR-MANCE?"

"Not a clue, sir."

"Mike would be very dangerous in the wrong hands. I just hope that he can survive aboard a real ship. A real ship is nothing like the training ships that he has been assigned,"

"I know, sir. I will send for him in the morning. Admiral Fantong, may I request a favor of STARCORE, sir."

"What's on your mind?"

"Perhaps we should have daily reports on CW01 Weatherspoon's progress aboard the USS PERFORMANCE for STARCORE security purposes and for psychological research."

"I concur, Vice Admiral Strauss and so it shall be done. Very well, dismissed."

Vice Admiral Strauss returned to his office and printed out the orders. He called the security desk and left word that Chief Warrant Officer Number One Mike Weatherspoon was to report to Vice Admiral Strauss' office first thing in the morning. CW01 Weatherspoon was to be ready for immediate departure and he was to be in full dress blue uniform with his hair tucked neatly inside his uniform. The security desk said that they would let CW01 Weatherspoon know in the morning.

The next morning, the security personnel informed CW01 Weatherspoon that he was needed in Vice Admiral Strauss' office. He was read the entire list of requirements. After packing up his uniforms and a few off duty clothes, he put on his dress blue uniform and reported to Vice Admiral Strauss' office. The vice admiral looked up at him as he walked into the room and waited for the door to shut behind him.

"CW01 Weatherspoon reporting as ordered, sir," said Mike, setting his bags down on the floor.

"Very well. CW01 Weatherspoon, I have here your orders from Admiral Fantong. He has seen fit to honor your request for a tour of duty aboard the USS PERFORMANCE. Here are your orders, please follow them," said Vice Admiral Strauss, handing Mike his duty orders disc, his personnel file disc, his medical disc and his personal effects and affairs disc.

"I will, sir."

"I hope you're ready for the real world. You have been living a sheltered life here at STARCORE headquarters. Those training ships are nothing compared to a real ship."

"I will take your advice seriously, Vice Admiral Strauss. What is the first order I must complete?"

"You are to report to the shuttle launch facilities in Colorado Springs, Colorado and get to Space Station 21 orbiting above the North Pole."

"Yes, sir."

"The rest of your orders are on the orders packet that I gave you. Please read them carefully with respect to what you are allowed and not allowed to do while aboard the USS PERFORMANCE."

"Yes, sir and thank you."

"Dismissed."

Mike picked up his bags and left the room. A few minutes later he was at the shuttle launching facility in Colorado Springs, Colorado. He found a shuttle that was stopping at Space Station 21. After he arrived aboard Space Station 21 and passed the small medical check, his next "shuttle" was actually the light battle cruiser USS TICONDEROGA. He reported there and fell asleep in the cabin assigned to him for the remainder of the journey. When he woke up, he showered and dressed back into his dress blue uniform.

Once the uniform was put on, he ate breakfast and then looked out at the stars going by. Mike could see several small space tugs coming alongside the USS TICONDEROGA. The ship made a sudden jerk and a voice was heard over the announcing system.

"USS TICONDEROGA, moored, shift colors."

CW01 Mike Weatherspoon picked up his bags and headed to the departure point. He had to wait for several shuttles before he was able to get onto one. The shuttlecraft flew to the main docking point for the large dry dock servicing all small and medium size STARCORE vessels. As the shuttlecraft rounded a corner, Mike caught a glimpse of the USS PERFORMANCE. When the shuttlecraft had landed, Mike walked off. He looked around and found a sign pointing to where the next shuttle for the USS PERFORMANCE would be departing from.

Mike stood there in his dress blue uniform, proudly sporting the balanced scales on the ends of the sleeves. To anyone who looked at him, they would know that he was a graduate of STARCORE Legal Corps Academy on Earth along with a commission as Chief Warrant Officer Number One. He looked down and saw the shuttlecraft coming to the air lock. Once the air lock was secured, Mike stepped aboard the shuttlecraft and it departed. A few minutes later, he was standing on the quarterdeck of the USS PERFORMANCE. He saluted the flags and turned to face the Officer of the Deck.

"Officer of the Deck, request permission to come aboard," said Mike as he saluted the Officer of the Deck.

"Permission granted, sir," replied the Officer of the Deck returning the salute.

"What can I do for you, sir?" asked the Officer of the Deck.

"I am the ship's new Legal Officer, Chief Warrant Officer Number One Mike Weatherspoon, Lieutenant Vrozneek."

"We have been expecting you, sir. If you will please follow the Petty Officer of the Watch, he will show you to your cabin."

"Sounds good to me."

The Petty Officer of the Watch escorted Mike Weatherspoon up to Deck 15. The former Legal Officer's quarters were now his. The Petty Officer of the Watch left Mike there in his cabin. The cabin was dirty and had webs hanging from the overhead. The cabin was not only dirty, but had an odor to it as well. Mike knew he had to clean up the cabin and went right to doing that duty. Once the cabin was cleaned up, however, the odor seemed to vanish.

After emptying his bags of his various uniforms, he turned on all the lights in the small cabin and looked around. Before walking outside of his cabin, he made sure that his long, blond hair was tucked neatly inside of his dress blue uniform. He walked outside his cabin and looked around the officer's quarters and noticed the map on the bulkhead. The map indicated that his cabin was on Deck 15; Section A. Mike spent his first night aboard the ship in utter amazement.

He had difficulty trying to find where to eat and where to shower. So instead of asking questions of anyone who might be walking by, he decided to just wander the ship. He followed some enlisted personnel to where they were gathered to eat. He couldn't remember saluting this many times in one day even aboard the training ships. As the day came to an end for him, he returned to his cabin and went to sleep.

CHAPTER 2

Mike woke up the next morning, shivering. His cabin was cold; in fact he thought he could see ice forming on the bulkheads of his cabin. He shivered again before finally deciding to wake up. As he stepped out of bed, he heard the announcement tone sound.

"Attention, all hands, there will be an all officers meeting in the wardroom at 0900 hours. Attention, all hands, there will be an all officers meeting in the wardroom at 0900 hours."

Mike put on his dress blue uniform, double-checked his hair to make sure that it was tucked neatly inside his uniform and then walked outside his cabin. It wasn't much warmer in the passageway than it was in his cabin.

After stepping onto the elevator and arriving at a much warmer deck, he followed some enlisted members to the mess hall. After eating a breakfast, which was interrupted by the cook with some forms for him to fill out on the meal, he looked up at the ship's clock, 0800 hours.

He watched another group of enlisted members and looked at all of them to find the one who was Damage Control. He found the engineering type, a Damage Controlman, First Class Petty Officer with a nametag attached to his red uniform that read FRONZ.

"Excuse me, DC1 Fronz, where is the ship's legal office located?" asked Mike.

"The ship's legal office is located on Deck 26, Section B, sir," he said, turning around and saluting Mike.

"Thank you," responded Mike, returning the salute.

Mike stepped into the elevator and rode the elevator down to Deck 26. He stepped off the elevator and was saluted several times. He located the map on the bulkhead that indicated where he was located. After reading the simple map, he started walking towards the ship's legal office. Upon finding the office, the door opened up and a very angry Legal Assistant, First Class Petty Officer, yelled at Mike as he threw a stack of paperwork down on the deck.

"As far as I'm concerned, when the new Legal Officer gets here, he can take over this case! That man is guilty as far as I'm concerned and should be executed!" he yelled, as he exited the door. The man didn't even salute Mike as he continued passed him towards the elevator.

"Attention on deck!" yelled the Legal Man Third Class Petty Officer.

The other three in the room stood up at attention. As the door shut behind Mike, he looked around the office and then down at the deck. The murder case was all over the deck. Mike reached down, picked it up and then set it down on the Legal Assistant Second Class Petty Officer's desktop.

"Carry on. I believe that was the 'I had it now you've got it' speech," said Mike, smiling.

"That, sir, was not right of him. You should write him up, sir," said the LA2, whose nametag read GRODER.

"You're right, what should I write him up for, LA2 Groder?" asked Mike.

"Under the STARCORE Uniform Code of Military Justice, LA1 Fracks violated Articles 11, 29 and 111."

"Granted, you're most astute, LA2 Groder. However, if you read the case studies that go with violating Article 11, he didn't really do that. But, he definitely violated Article 29, Failure to Salute an Officer. As far as violating Article 111, he might have done it, but you would have to prove intent," replied Mike, reaching out and shaking the LA2's right hand.

"You must be the ship's new Legal Officer, sir," said LA2 Groder.

"I am. My name is Mike Weatherspoon, Chief Warrant Officer Number One," said Mike, shaking everybody else's hands.

"I am Legal Man Third Class Petty Officer Bjork. Everyone around here considers me a lunatic," he said, shaking Mike's left hand.

"Why are you considered a lunatic?" asked Mike.

"Because, until you came along, I have tried to be a lawyer. Sometimes I win and sometimes I lose, sir."

"Well, once I get settled in down here, we should go over your cases and see what went wrong."

"I would like that very much, sir."

"I am Legal Assistant Third Class Petty Officer Monks. I do very well with research, but a court-martial or trial scares me to death. I don't do well in front of others, sir," she said, shaking his right hand.

"Well, LA3 Monks, I will be happy to work with you on that issue. Maybe sometime we can get you over this issue."

"Thank you, sir."

"Well, I have to go to an all officers meeting in the wardroom at 0900 hours. Can any of you tell me where the wardroom is located?"

"Yes, sir. The wardroom is located on Deck 9, Section C."

"Thank you, LN3. Once I am out of this meeting, I will return here and we can start going over the cases at hand."

Mike turned around and walked out the door. He summoned the elevator and noticed it was quite full. He managed to squeeze himself into the back and noticed that, luckily, someone else was going to Deck 9 as well. When he and this other person stepped off the elevator, Mike could hear the noise coming from the wardroom.

He stepped into the wardroom and the entire wardroom was suddenly speechless. He looked around the wardroom and found an empty seat not too far from the captain. Mike took the seat and the wardroom stayed quiet.

"Good morning, Ladies and Gentlemen. This morning, I received our orders from STARCORE. Operations Officer, would you please brief everyone on our mission," said Captain Powers, taking his seat and looking down at the dress blue uniform. When he saw the balanced scales, he knew that this was the cyborg Admiral Fantong had mentioned.

"Thank you, sir. Our mission is to make surveys of a non-explored galaxy classified by 20th century Earth as NGC-7628. This galaxy is in the Charlie Quadrant within the Pegasus Constellation," said the Operations Officer.

"Science Officer, is your department ready for this mission?" asked the captain.

"Yes, sir. I have been outfitted with the latest in probes. All of my crew are ready, sir," replied the Science Officer.

"Good. Personnel Officer, see to it that all departments make a readiness report for getting underway," said the captain.

"Yes, sir."

"Now, computer, secure this room," announced the captain, as he stood up.

"Room secured, Captain Powers," responded the computer's voice.

"Ladies and Gentlemen, we are part of a great STARCORE experiment. Our new Legal Officer for the ship has arrived. Chief Warrant Officer Number One Mike Weatherspoon has come to us from STARCORE Legal Academy and is a cyborg," said the captain.

"In other words, he is a machine, captain?" asked the Weapons Officer.

"Not a machine, commander. I am, by STARCORE regulations, half human, half machine. I am the best of both worlds. I have superior intelligence coupled with reflexes three times faster than a human and I have five times the physical strength of a human," replied Mike, callously.

"Sir, I don't think this was a wise decision to bring this thing aboard this ship," replied the Personnel Officer.

John didn't say anything right away. Instead, he wanted to see how the young chief warrant officer would handle himself. John made sure to take careful mental notes that would be transferred to the required STARCORE psychological daily activity report.

"Are you afraid of me, sir?" asked Mike.

"No, not personally, but I don't want you to start telling me how to run my office, either."

"Personnel Officer, I have been specifically ordered by Admiral Fantong not to interfere with any of the ship's functions. I am solely responsible for being the ship's Legal Officer and this is my sole title. Captain Powers, I believe you will find that Vice Admiral Strauss has a special set of instructions for you, sir."

"I was made aware of such special instructions," replied John, still taking notes.

"Mr. Weatherspoon, do you have any hand-to-hand combat training?" asked the ship's Security Officer, without hesitation.

"Yes, sir. I am trained in Ninjitsu and hold current qualifications in laser pistol, laser rifle and mortar training. I also hold current qualifications in damage control and hostile planetary survival."

"Great, could you possibly train some of my boarding party personnel at some point?"

"I would love to, sir. If the captain will authorize such," said Mike, turning to look at the captain.

"Granted. I think we can all learn a lot from Mr. Weatherspoon," replied the captain.

"I gather, captain, that we are the only ones to know of his uniqueness. Are we under orders not to divulge his uniqueness?" asked the Medical Officer.

"Yes, that is right. However, both Admiral Fantong's instructions and Vice Admiral Strauss' instructions are clearly stated. If the question is asked of him directly, then he is required to answer," said John.

"And, of course, you're right, captain. I want everyone at this table to know, before anyone gets any crazy ideas, that I am a thinking, feeling cyborg. Unlike other cyborgs that have been created artificially in the many STARCORE laboratories in the galaxy, I cry, laugh, joke, get sick and have emotions and feelings, just like a human," said Mike.

"Captain, this might be a problem in the medical community. I don't have any formal training in cyborgs, sir," said the Medical Officer.

"You are to only treat his physical medical conditions, such as sickness, etc. We have Cybernetic Technicians who will take care of the rest," replied the captain.

"Mr. Weatherspoon, since you are of both worlds, I would like to chat with you when you get the chance," said the Command Chaplain Rear Admiral Lower Half Robbins.

"I would like that very much, too, sir. Captain Powers, I was not aware that your ship had a flag officer aboard," said Mike.

"He is staff position and therefore cannot assume command of this vessel. He serves as my conscience."

"I see. Thank you all for allowing me this opportunity to be aboard a wonderful vessel," said Mike.

"Mr. Weatherspoon, when we get underway, I will make arrangements for an orientation. Is there anything else you have to say?"

"One thing. Chief Engineer, my cabin was so cold this morning that I could see ice forming on the bulkheads, could we do something about the heat?"

"Yes, sir. Captain, since there was no one on Deck 15, I ordered the environmental controls turned all the way down, please forgive me, sir," replied the Chief Engineer.

"I didn't think you did that intentionally. I figured it had to do with the fact that the deck looks like it has not been inhabited in some time," replied Mike.

"I will reactivate the environmental controls within the hour. Captain, my department is ready to get underway, request permission to switch from space dock power to ship's power."

"Permission granted. All personnel are dismissed except the XO and Mr. Weatherspoon."

The wardroom emptied out quickly. Once everyone was gone, the captain ordered coffee for everyone and then looked straight at Mr. Weatherspoon. Mr. Weatherspoon was a little nervous with this at first, but soon the nervousness wore off.

"As the ship's new Legal Officer, you have a very ugly case on your hands with the one crewmember who shot the other one in the back, killing him," said John.

"I understand that this is a difficult case for some members of your crew, sir," said Mike.

"It is, indeed. However, we all wear the same uniform around here. I will have the Supply Officer deliver uniforms to your cabin. Please change into the uniform of the day before assuming the duties as the Legal Officer," said the XO.

"I will, sir. Now, about that murder case, I would like to get started on it right away."

"Do your best, Mr. Weatherspoon. Oh, by the way, I understand that you had a run in with LA1 Fracks this morning?" asked John.

"Yes, I did, sir."

"He should be written up, you know," prodded John.

"Written up for what, too much testosterone? I don't remember too much testosterone being illegal aboard STARCORE vessels, sir. Unless the ship's medical officer has knowledge of a crewmember that has possession of a controlled/illegal substance, aboard a STARCORE vessel/shore facility. If you can prove that is such the case, I will not hesitate to have him prosecuted, sir."

"You're right, please get changed and report for duty," said XO.

"Yes, sir."

Mike left the wardroom, as did John and the XO. Mike waited in his cabin for about half an hour before the uniforms arrived. Mike put on his uniform and attached the appropriate accoutrements to the uniform before tucking his hair inside the black with green stripes down the sleeves and pants coverall style of uniform.

The end of the sleeves and the lapels indicated that he was the ship's Legal Officer with the balanced scales with a quill crossing the middle part of the scales on the right side of the uniform. The left side of the uniform had his rank sewn into the sleeve and the left lapel contained a metal version of the rank. The rank marking consisted of a gold bar with three, evenly spaced, breaks to indicate that he was a chief warrant officer number one. He noticed that his cabin and the passageway were getting much warmer now.

He returned to the office and found everyone busy with getting ready to get underway. He helped out as best he could, even though there were some things that were happening that didn't happen on the training vessels. The announcement tone sounded.

"Attention, all hands, attention, all hands, prepare to shift from space dock power to ship's power in 15 minutes. Place all electronic and electrical gear in standby mode."

"Are you going to write up LA1 Fracks, sir?" asked LN3 Bjork.

"No, I don't think so. You see, he was very frustrated and very annoyed because he knew, by STARCORE regulations, that he could not sign the paperwork as the Legal Officer. I will talk with him about his behavior a little later on this week. Right now, however, we have a murder case to deal with," said Mike.

"Yes, sir. What would you like to do first, sir?" asked the LN3.

"Please get me the file on this case. I would like to review it while we are getting ready to commence our mission," said Mike.

"Yes, sir."

The LN3 returned a short time later with the file. The LA2 had completely put the file back together. As Mike reviewed the case, he saw some things that were probably going to let the crewmember plead not guilty to the charge of First Degree Murder and either request a full military tribunal or request a court-martial. Other options included the crewmember could plead guilty to Second Degree Murder, Involuntary Manslaughter or Criminally Negligent Homicide.

Mike was reviewing the case when the lights flickered a little and then came back on again. The ship suddenly shook and the announcement tone sounded. Mike looked around his office and the desktop finding a coffee cup embellished with the STARCORE seal and the seal of the USS PERFORMANCE.

"Underway, shift colors. The USS PERFORMANCE is underway."

Mike raised his eyebrows a little when LA1 Fracks came back into the office. LA1 Fracks looked at Mike and stood at attention in front of him. After rendering proper salutes, Mike stood up and shook Fracks' left hand.

"At ease, LA1 Fracks. How long have you been working on this murder case?" asked Mike.

"From the beginning, sir. I would like to apologize for my behavior earlier today; it was inexcusable, sir."

"I'll agree with that, and I won't be writing you up this time. Everybody has their bad days and needs forgiveness. Tell me, what have you found out so far?"

"I think he is guilty, sir and deserves to die," replied the LA1.

"So, you think he did it intentionally, then?"

"Yes, sir. From the reports that are contained in the file and from his own testimony, he did intentionally discharge his laser pistol into the back of his fellow crewmember, killing him."

"Where is the accused located?" asked Mike.

"Deck AA, Section B, Cell 1224, maximum-security, sir."

"How long has he been there?"

"188 days, so far, sir."

"Has the accused made any statements to you or to anyone else?"

"Only to me, sir. The accused originally stated that he didn't think he discharged his weapon but, then, he later stated he couldn't remember if he had discharged his weapon. I think he's guilty, sir."

"I'll keep that in mind. So the accused has been locked up in maximum-security for 188 days and has had no contact with family, friends or any legal representation, is that correct?"

"Not exactly, sir. He has had limited contact with friends and family and he has had contact with me as his legal counsel. But, now that you are here, I will relinquish that right to you, sir."

"Thank you, LA1, I appreciate that. Now, where is the evidence being held?"

"Deck BB, Section A, Bin 12, sir."

"I would like to see the evidence being held against my client."

"Yes, sir. I will go get it right now."

"Wait, aren't you forgetting to file the chain of custody for the evidence?"

"I don't have the authority to obtain the chain of custody form and sign for the evidence. I have the ship's Security Officer accompany me to the evidence locker. He watches me as I inspect and handle the evidence."

"I understand that was how you had to do it before, but now that I am here, we will follow the rules. The main reason why, is, if a person is guilty, then I don't want to defend them. If they are innocent, then I will aggressively defend them to the very end."

"I hear you, sir. I will obtain STARCORE Form 0056.7D, Chain of Custody for Evidence."

"Good, when you're done with that, I want to see the evidence."

"Yes, sir."

LA1 Fracks left the room and returned with the electronic version of the form. Mike signed the block allowing the evidence to be removed and brought back to the Legal Office. When LA1 Fracks had left, Mike stood up and walked out of the office. He took along his coffee cup and returned a short time later to find the evidence he had asked for on his desktop. Mike sat down and went through the evidence.

The evidence consisted of the Mark VII laser pistol, the spatter pattern from the impact of the laser bolt hit and a few other items, including the coroner's report. Mike read the report and saw something that didn't quite fit the requirements of intentionally killing someone.

He then looked at the laser pistol power pack report. The report indicated only one discharge. The pictures showed burned flesh on both the back and the front of the body. Mike put all the evidence back into the evidence bag and instructed LA1 Fracks to return the evidence to the evidence locker. Next, Mike looked up at the clock and saw that it was almost time for lunch.

After returning from lunch, Mike thought more about the case and how something was amiss in the situation. He looked over his desktop and saw LA3 Monks sitting at her desk going over some legal forms that the crew had signed earlier.

"LA3 Monks, would you please prepare evidence tags for the evidence in this case?" asked Mike.

"Yes, sir."

She started to fill out evidence tags and then took them down to the evidence storage bin. When she had returned, Mike stood up and looked down at LN3 Bjork. He looked up at Mike.

"Is there something I can do for you, sir?" he asked.

"Yes, please fill out STARCORE Form 0005.11A. I request to see the accused and offer my services as his counsel."

"Yes, sir."

Bjork electronically filled out the form and submitted it to the ship's Personnel Officer for processing. When the Personnel Officer had signed off on it, the form was sent to both the ship's Security Officer and ship's Security Force Commander, Colonel Raddison, who was guarding the accused in a maximum-security cell. The form came back signed and Bjork handed the electronic form to Mike. Mike took the form and headed to the ship's brig. Upon arrival, Security Force Personnel challenged Mike.

"Who are you and what is your business, sir?" asked the ensign, who was serving as the Brig's Duty Officer.

"I am Chief Warrant Officer Number One Mike Weatherspoon. I am the ship's Legal Officer and I have permission to see the accused," said Mike, handing over the electronic clipboard.

"I see, sir. The accused is in cell 1224. Please follow me," said the ensign as he led Mike down a long passageway. Mike could hear the electrified door of the maximum-security cell.

The ensign opened the door to cell 1224. The accused stood up and stood at attention. When Mike had entered into the cell, the ensign stepped back out of the cell and closed the door. Mike knew that all he had to do was to push the call button on the inside of the cell on the bulkhead to his right to summon the ensign back. The accused, as Mike looked him over, was a Master-At-Arms First Class Petty Officer.

"At ease MA1, I am Chief Warrant Officer Number One Mike Weatherspoon. I am the ship's Legal Officer. I am here to offer my services to you as the accused," said Mike, shaking the man's left hand.

"You probably think that I am guilty, don't you?" asked the man, with a certain shakiness to his voice.

"No, I don't think you killed your fellow crewmember intentionally. I have read your statements and they seem to indicate to me that you may not exactly remember what happened."

"Yes, sir, that is correct. My finger was on the trigger and the weapon went off and that's about all that I clearly remember, sir."

"You're right about that inculpatory evidence. Your fingerprint was on the trigger and the weapon's power pack indicates a single discharge. Do you want me to represent you in any way?"

"Yes, sir. What are my options?"

"Right now, STARCORE wants to put you to death for First Degree Murder. However, I need to know what you are willing to do, or want to do, at this point. Have you been read your rights, been given a copy of them and did you sign your rights as they were read to you?"

"Yes, sir."

"Having these rights still in your mind, do you wish to cooperate with me and STARCORE to reach a conclusion for these events?"

"Yes, sir."

"How do you plead?"

"Not guilty, sir."

"Do you want a full trial, a court-martial or military tribunal?"

"Court-martial, sir."

"So it will be. According to your statement, you say the weapon went off when you entered the engine room of the USS SEA TIGER, is that correct?"

"Yes, sir. I don't remember if I saw something, or if I tripped, or what happened. All I can tell you is, that, on that particular law enforcement operation, my weapon went off, sir."

"Was it customary for your weapon to be out of its holster on these types of missions?"

"No, sir. We, the boarding party, that is, were told by the ship's Security Officer that the ship's sensors had detected a life form aboard the ship we were boarding,"

"Was this life form, perhaps, dangerous?" asked Mike.

"Yes, sir. According to the ship's Security Officer, the life form was classified as dangerous to human life."

"What happened next?"

"We boarded the ship and that's when my weapon went off. Sir, I don't want to end my 18 year STARCORE career by being executed."

"I will do everything I can to salvage your career. I'm glad we had this little talk. I will forward, up the chain of command, your request for a court-martial. I want you to get some rest now," said Mike, pushing the call button.

Mike left the brig and went back to his office. It was well after 2000 hours by that time and his office staff had gone to bed already. He closed the office door and locked it up. He went to bed in a much warmer cabin this time and slept until the next morning.

Chapter 3

M ike woke up early the next morning, took a shower and dressed into his uniform. After making sure that his hair had been tucked neatly inside the uniform, he went to the wardroom and had breakfast. When breakfast was completed, he went to the office and found it already occupied by LN3 Bjork. No one else was in the office. Mike sat down at his desk and started looking back over the report. After a few minutes, the rest of the legal office showed up and they all went to work quietly.

"LA3 Monks, would you please come see me. I wish to talk to you," said Mike.

"Yes, sir," she said, entering into the office with her electronic recorder for taking notes. The door silently closed behind her.

"You're my research person, if my memory serves me correctly. Am I right?" asked Mike.

"Yes, sir."

"Good. I want you to find me all the information you can on the STARCORE Mark VII issue laser pistol and report back to me when you have the information."

"Yes, sir."

"LN3 Bjork, would you please come into my office," said Mike, loudly.

"Yes, sir," he replied, as he took his electronic note recorder into the office. He entered the office and sat down in the chair directly in front of Mike.

"You're the one who wants to be the lawyer, right?" asked Mike.

"Yes, sir."

"I want you to find me three recent court cases dealing with first degree murder where a STARCORE issue, Mark VII laser pistol was used. When you have found those three cases, I want you to give me a legal briefing on them."

"Yes, sir."

"When you leave, please send in LA2 Groder."

"Yes, sir."

LA2 Groder entered the office and sat down. His electronic note recorder was ready to go.

"LA2 Groder, I want you to assemble me a list of the witnesses to the incident. I may want to talk to them prior to the court-martial."

"Yes, sir. Is there anything else?"

"No, not right now. I want you to send in LA1 Fracks."

"Yes, sir."

LA1 Fracks entered the office. His electronic note recorder was ready to go. He sat down in the chair directly facing Mike. Mike stood up and started walking around the small office before speaking.

"LA1 Fracks, I want you to accompany me today around the ship and to act as my extra set of eyes when we talk to people."

"Yes, sir."

"I want you to write the question down that I ask the person and then I want you to write the answer they give as well."

"Yes, sir. Is there anything else?"

"Not now, maybe later. Please send in LN3 Bjork if he is out there."

"Yes, sir."

LN3 Bjork entered the office. He sat down in the chair and waited for Mike to issue instructions. Bjork had his electronic note recorder ready to go. Mike stood up from behind his desk and started pacing the small office. After a few minutes of this, Mike sat back down.

"LN3 Bjork, would you please fill out STARCORE Form 0012.1A Request for General Court-Martial by the Accused."

"Yes, sir. What is the plea?"

"The accused has entered a plea of not guilty on the formal charge of First Degree Murder. We request a General Court-Martial be convened in accordance with STARCORE Court-Martial Manual Paragraph 98, Sections 1-4. Before you send the form up to the captain for his signature, give it to me for a review."

"Yes, sir."

A few minutes later, LN3 Bjork entered the office with the electronic form filled out. Mike reviewed the form and signed it, signifying that he saw the form and that it was correct. The form's next stop was the XO and then the captain. The XO took the form, reviewed it and then handed it to the captain. After the captain signed it, he handed it back to the XO who returned it to the LN3. LN3 Bjork returned to the office in the afternoon with the form signed.

"I will inform the accused that his plea has been entered and that the process of selecting the officers and enlisted members for the court-martial is beginning," said Mike.

Mike left the office in the late afternoon and saw the prisoner. Once Mike was inside his cell, the door was closed and the accused stood before Mike.

"Your plea has been entered in regards to the charge of First Degree Murder and the commanding officer of this vessel has agreed to your request for a court-martial. Here is your copy of the paperwork," said Mike, handing the man an electronic copy of the signed form.

"Thank you, sir. Now, when is this court-martial going to take place?"

"In accordance with the STARCORE Court-Martial Manual, Paragraph 23 clearly states that the court-martial must be convened no later than 270 days from the date of the plea entry, or no later than 180 days from the date of arrest."

"What do you think is going to happen, sir?"

"I don't know. If the captain waits too long, then the 270 days will pass and you're free. The charges must be dropped in accordance with the 6th and 14th Amendments to the U.S. Constitution. Also, STARCORE regulations require similar actions. Right now, you're beyond the 180 day limit."

"Thank you, sir, for defending me on this charge."

"Not a problem. I just hope that something comes up to help your situation in the near future. Do you need anything?"

"No, sir, I am fine."

"Very well, until next time," said Mike as he pressed the call button.

Mike left the ship's brig once again. When he had returned to his office, both the captain and XO were standing there. Mike smiled and then pointed the way to his office. Everyone filed into the office and the door shut behind Mike. Once they were all inside, the XO took the offensive.

"You mean to tell me that the accused has requested a court-martial and has pleaded not guilty to the crime?!" yelled the XO.

"Yes, XO, that is exactly what is meant by that form. In accordance with the STARCORE Court-Martial Manual, that is his right, sir."

"I don't believe it. How can you expect to get your client off with a court-martial?" asked the XO.

"I am not going to discuss the defensive tactics that I am going to use. What I expect is that this ship comply with the regulations set forth in the STARCORE Court-Martial Manual and give my client his day in court."

"How long do we have to convene this general court-martial?" asked John.

"About another 80 days, sir. The general court-martial must begin by day 270. However, since there were some legal STARCORE holidays within the original arrest timeframe, I will give you an extra five days."

"Very well. XO, assemble members of the crew, both officers and enlisted, that meet the STARCORE jury requirements."

"Sir, ship's crew would not meet the eligibility requirements."

"Why not?"

"In accordance with the 6th, 14th and 35th Amendments to the U.S. Constitution and in accordance with the STARCORE Court-Martial Manual, Article 44, Section 16, Paragraphs 1-20, my client could not possibly receive a fair trial aboard this vessel."

"I understand, Warrant Officer Weatherspoon. May I please have some time to obtain the necessary personnel? I request that this general court-martial take place aboard this vessel for operational reasons," said John.

"Warrant, where can this general court-martial be held?" asked the XO.

"The general court-martial can be held in any quiet place of the ship. I must still protest that the accused would not receive a fair trial aboard this ship."

"Would a battle room be sufficient?" asked the XO.

"Yes, sir, it will meet the requirements, XO."

"Then, captain, I will prepare Battle Room Six to serve as the court room."

"Very well. Let me find the necessary personnel."

"I will await your answer, sir."

The captain and the XO left the office. When they had stepped out into the passageway, LA3 Monks knocked on the doorframe. Mike looked up and smiled.

"Come on in, LA3 Monks."

"Thank you, sir. I have downloaded all the information about the former STARCORE issue Mark VII laser pistol. Nothing in the documents that I downloaded from STARCORE were unusual," she said, handing Mike the electronic report.

Mike reviewed the report and then handed it back to LA3 Monks. He looked in Monks' direction and thought for a little while. Mike then asked to see the report again and reread it. There, on the last page, was a keynote that Mike could use, since he would be playing defense attorney when the court-martial convened. The STARCORE issue Mark VII laser pistol was pulled from service four months BEFORE the incident, for some reason, which was classified.

"You did a good job today. When you leave, I want you to send in LN3 Bjork."

"Yes, sir."

LN3 Bjork stepped into the office a few minutes later. He stood ready to record any notes with his electronic note recorder. He sat down in front of Mike as Mike thought for a few minutes. Finally, Mike stood up and started walking around the office.

"LN3 Bjork, I asked you to find me three recent murder cases and how those cases turned out. What did you find?" asked Mike.

"The first case I came across was labeled 1011 U.S. 998, *STARCORE V. Wainright.* In that case, STARCORE accused Commander Wainright of killing one of his own crewmembers with a Mark VII, STARCORE issue laser pistol. He was acquitted of the charges. His attorney convinced the court-martial judge and jury that the weapon had inadvertently discharged due to being jarred hard when the ship lost her port stabilizers. As the ship listed to port, the commander was thrown against the bulkhead which caused the weapon to discharge."

"Good, what was the next case you found?"

"The second case I came across was labeled 1011 U.S. 999, *STARCORE et.al V. Saturn Weapons manufacturing.* In this case, the STARCORE issue, Mark VII laser pistol had actually blown up in the operators hand, killing her and several of her crewmembers. The amount of damage was substantial and caused STARCORE to have to look for another weapons supplier for small arms."

"Good. What's next?"

"The third case I came across is still in the court system. It has not made its way to the U.S. Supreme Court to be heard or voted on, yet. The case number is 11-009, *Roberts et.al V. Saturn Weapons manufacturing.* Mr. Roberts, a security guard at the Saturn plant, was accused of killing a burglar with a Mark VII laser pistol. While the weapon was set on a stun setting, the weapon somehow was recalibrated to the kill setting. The Saturn Company acknowledged that the pistol may have been defective, but fired the man anyway."

"Great job. Now, if you were in my position as the defense attorney, what exculpatory evidence would you want to present to the jury and judge?"

"Something that might prove that my client was a victim of circumstances beyond their control."

"Right, now think about what evidence I would look at, as the prosecutor, that would prove my client committed the crime."

"As a prosecutor, I would show the judge and the jury the flight deck tapes and the evidence of the weapon's discharge and the dead body."

"Good, now, what other exculpatory evidence would be needed to produce, say, just a little doubt into the minds of the judge and jury, that my client was actually innocent?"

"The fact that the weapon was pulled from service before this incident because it was defective in some manner. I might look for other evidence of something that went wrong down there, in the engineering spaces of the USS SEA TIGER, beyond my client's control. I might review the flight recorders of the USS SEA TIGER, sir."

"Excellent thinking. LN3, when you leave here, send in LA2 Groder, would you please?"

"Yes, sir."

A moment later, LA2 Groder was standing in front of Mike. Mike looked up and waited for the door to shut before speaking to LA2 Groder.

"Yes, sir, what can I do for you?" he asked, holding his electronic note recorder at the ready.

"I need a seizure warrant for the USS SEA TIGER's In-Deck, Engineering/Engine Room Flight Recorders from 8 July 2112 at 1200 hours to 8 July 2112 at 1400 hours. I also will need another seizure warrant for the portside passageway in-deck flight recorder, for the same dates and times, leading into the engine room."

"Yes, sir. May I ask who is going to sign these seizure warrants?"

"The ship's Security Officer, the ship's Personnel Officer or the ship's Weapons Officer may sign the warrants."

"Yes, sir. I will get on this right away."

"When you leave, please send in LA3 Monks."

"Yes, sir."

LA3 Monks, once again, entered the office. After the door shut behind her, she looked at Mike with her electronic note recorder ready. Mike looked up and then back down at the desktop.

"LA3 Monks, I want you to alter your search pattern. I want you to find the exact reason why the Saturn Weapons Manufacturing Company's Mark VII Laser Pistol was pulled from service."

"Yes, sir."

"Dismissed."

LA3 Monks left the office. LA3 Monks returned a short time later with a very worried look on her face. In her electronic clipboard's memory was a restricted STARCORE military research file. The file contained the reason why the Mark VII Laser Pistol had been pulled from service.

The weapon was pulled from service because it could be unintentionally discharged if the weapon was bumped or jarred. Also, merely pulling the weapon out of its holster could change the settings. Mike looked up as Monks locked the door.

"Mr. Weatherspoon, I think I have committed a crime in obtaining this information, sir," said Monks.

"Well, I'm glad you let me know and I'm glad you locked the door," said Mike.

"Sir, the Mark VII Laser Pistol was pulled from service and replaced by the Mark IX Laser Pistol because the Mark VII pistol was found to be defective in both design and construction," said Monks.

"Defective in what way?"

"Well, that's where the military research restricted file comes into play. You see, I'm not supposed to have access to that kind of a file, yet it was downloaded with the rest of the Saturn Weapons Manufacturing Company's data."

"Oh, I see. Well, case law states that if you end up with possession of information that is beyond your security clearance level, you can be charged with committing espionage. However, I believe this may be some sort of administrative error."

"That's good to know, sir."

"However, this piece of information gives me a big piece of this puzzle we're working on right now. You're dismissed."

"Yes, sir."

"Please send in LN3 Bjork."

"Yes, sir."

Monks left as Bjork entered. After the door shut behind Bjork, Mike looked up.

"Have you had a chance to think of other evidence that you might need as a defense attorney?" asked Mike.

"Yes, sir. I would think that the ship's sensor logs should be looked at, sir."

"Why?"

"I was part of that boarding party. Once we were aboard, my party went to the bridge to check and make a copy of their manifest logs. After obtaining a copy of their manifest logs, I returned to the ship and that's when I found out about the murder."

"When you leave, send in LA1 Fracks."

"Yes, sir."

Fracks entered the office. He stood at attention in front of Mike. Mike narrowed his eyes a little before returning them to their normal position.

"Mr. Fracks, would you please obtain a seizure warrant for the USS PERFORMANCE's sensor records from 1045 hours on 8 July 2112 to 1405 hours on 8 July 2112."

"Yes, sir."

"When you have submitted that seizure warrant request, would you please grab your electronic note recorder and accompany me to interview various people aboard the ship?"

"Yes, sir."

Fracks left the office as Mike, seeing that it was about lunchtime, decided to go to lunch. When he had returned from lunch, he found Monks looking worried again.

"Is there something wrong, Monks?" asked Mike.

"Yes, sir. Captain Manning is on the video link for you, sir. He wants to discuss terms of MA1 Masterson's court-martial."

"I understand. Please have Fracks wait for me in the outer office, while I am on the video link."

"Yes, sir."

Mike entered his office to find Captain Manning on his video screen. Mike sat down in front of the screen and smiled as he looked at Captain Manning.

"Greetings, Warrant Officer Weatherspoon. I was calling to see if we could plea bargain this case and let your client go with a dishonorable discharge."

"No go, sir. We have requested a general court-martial."

"You think your client is innocent? Your client killed his own crewmember in cold blood. If you don't take the plea bargain, I will charge your client with all sorts of things."

"Like what?"

"First Degree Murder, Second Degree Murder, Manslaughter and Criminally Negligent Homicide, for starters."

"What kind of plea bargain?"

"If you're client pleads guilty to the charge of First Degree Murder, I will make arrangements for life in prison without parole. How about that?"

"No go, sir. You have barely enough evidence to support the murder one charge. My client may plead guilty to Criminally Negligent Homicide for a two-year prison term and a general discharge."

"No way. I will not let a murderer get away with killing his own crewmember by pleading guilty to a lesser crime."

"Then I will see you at the court-martial, sir."

Before Captain Manning could say anything more, Mike terminated the conversation. Mike rose up out of his chair and entered the outer office. Mike motioned for Fracks to follow him out of the office. Fracks grabbed his electronic note recorder and followed. Once they were in the elevator, Mike looked at Fracks.

"Fracks, STARCORE is going to charge MA1 Masterson with a whole bunch of charges.

"Are they going to win, sir?" asked Fracks.

"I don't think so, STARCORE's case is a little weak. Who is first on my list of people to talk to?"

"The Weapons Officer."

"Very well."

Mike and Fracks entered the office of the ship's Weapons Officer. He was completing up some paperwork. Once he saw Fracks and Mike standing in his office, he stood up and shut the door. He returned to his seat and looked up at Mike.

"What can I do for you, Warrant Officer Weatherspoon?" asked the Weapons Officer.

"I would like to ask some questions of you, about the incident that caused my client to be arrested. LA1 Fracks will be taking notes if you have no objections, sir," said Mike.

"I have no objections," he replied.

"Good. Sir, were you aware that the Mark VII Laser Pistol may have had some problems?" asked Mike.

"Yes and no. Yes, I was aware, from my own observations, that the laser pistol was capable of doing odd things of its own accord. No, STARCORE did not directly address my concerns over the laser pistol's safety."

"So STARCORE ignored your observations on the laser pistol?"

"Yes, sir, that is essentially correct, that is why STARCORE now has the new Mark IX models."

"Thank you for your time, could I please have a copy of your STARCORE requests for the file?"

"You certainly can. Off the record, I think your client was the victim of the most terrible set of circumstances."

"Well, thank you, sir. I will be looking forward to seeing you at the court-martial."

"Then you have officially subpoenaed me to appear?"

"That is correct, sir."

"I will be there."

Mike and Fracks left the Weapons Officer's office and proceeded to their next stop, the Science Department. Upon arrival, Mike and Fracks noticed that there were a lot of experiments going on at one time. All the labs were in use and it took Mike and Fracks a few minutes to find the Science Officer. The Science Officer was not very cooperative and evaded Mike's questions. Mike terminated the questioning early in the conversation and instead, handed the Science Officer an electronic subpoena.

Mike and Fracks' next stop was to the quarters where the dead person had berthed. Mike looked around the berthing compartment. It was neat, tidy and clean. The dead man's personal effects had been sent home to Earth to his relatives there. As Mike and Fracks turned around to leave the berthing compartment, they came face-to-face with the dead man's best friend.

"Who are you?" asked the man.

"Chief Warrant Officer Number One Mike Weatherspoon, this is Legal Assistant First Class Petty Officer Fracks, we were just about to leave," said Mike, realizing that a confrontation was in the works. Mike was quickly thinking about how to defuse this escalating situation.

"Oh, you're the new Legal Officer, sir. The same person that is defending the murderer of my best friend. That MA1 Masterson is guilty as far as I'm concerned. Only a coward would shoot someone in the back. I would appreciate it if you would just leave, sir," said the Yeoman Third Class Petty Officer with a nametag that read JOHNSON.

"You're right, only a coward would shoot someone in the back, YN3 Johnson. I just came by here to get a feel for the deceased. You two must have been close friends, I gather."

"Yes, sir, but I asked you to leave, sir."

"Yes, I know you asked me to leave. Mr. Fracks, will you please come with me."

"Yes, sir."

As they left the berthing compartment and stepped onto the elevator, Fracks looked at Mike. Mike looked over at Fracks as they stepped off the elevator and headed towards the office. Once they were in the office, Mike silenced Fracks from saying anything until after the office door was shut and locked.

"YN3 Johnson is going to be our worst enemy," announced Mike.

"I kind of thought so, sir. His body language and facial expressions made it seem that we were his worst enemy."

"Well, please download your recorder and seal up the files. Get some sleep, because, any day now, we will be receiving the official list of charges on the accused."

"Yes, sir. What are you going to do about that potentially hostile witness?"

"Treat him with respect and try to let the jury see that I make this witness very nervous."

"Yes, sir. Good night, sir."

"Good night, Fracks."

Everyone else had left the office when Fracks stepped out of the outer office. Mike walked out a few minutes later and made a mental note to himself to speak with the accused in the morning. Mike went to bed but didn't sleep very well at all. When the alarm clock went off next to him on the nightstand, Mike had just woken up from a flashback from being aboard the USS SCORPION. He could feel the searing heat from being blasted in the back, legs and arms.

CHAPTER 4

Mike went to the wardroom for breakfast. He had a quick bite to eat and then approached the captain. John looked up at the same time as the XO.

"Captain Powers, I forgot to ask you what the uniform of the day is going to be for the court-martial," said Mike.

"Dress blue with full accoutrements," replied John.

"What's the plan, Mike?" asked the XO.

"Captain Laguer, my plan is complex. I must show that my client is innocent of the charges and that STARCORE may be negligent."

"I believe that this will be an interesting case, Mike. Are we on the list of witnesses?" asked the XO again.

"Yes, sir. A couple of other officers have been subpoenaed in addition to some of the crew," replied Mike.

"Can I ask a question about what was meant by the comment 'STARCORE may be negligent'?" asked John.

"I have a theory that the murderer may not have known that the STARCORE issued laser pistol, in this case the Mark VII, was known by STARCORE to be defective."

"Chief Warrant Officer Number One Weatherspoon?" asked the Communications Officer.

"Yes?" answered Mike, turning around to face her.

"I have here a priority message for you from STARCORE in regards to your request for a court-martial," she said, handing the electronic clipboard to Mike.

"Thank you," said Mike as he took the clipboard.

He left the wardroom looking over the first part of the message. The message was in three sections. The first section was the official announcement that the court-martial would be held aboard the USS PERFORMANCE inside Battle Room Six and included the start time. There was also information on the uniform of the day for the court-martial, the list of witnesses and Motion of Discovery request.

The second section contained the list of charges and what the accused pleaded on those charges. The third section indicated that the computer had randomly chosen a jury pool as well as the judge and prosecutor. Mike noticed that the list contained both officer and enlisted personnel. When the elevator stopped, he stepped off and walked down the passageway to his office.

He entered the office and found everyone totally silent. They looked up at him as he walked into the office. Monks looked up at Mike and spoke first to break the uneasy silence.

"We understand that there was a priority message from STARCORE to you, sir," she said.

"Yes, I have the message here on the message clipboard. The court-martial is to start tomorrow morning at 0800 hours. Uniform of the day for the court-martial will be dress blues."

"Yes, sir. In your absence, I complied with the Motion of Discovery Request from the prosecutor. A copy of all the evidence, interviews etc., with the exception of the hard physical evidence, was sent to Captain Manning a few minutes ago," said Bjork.

"Very good, Mr. Bjork. Miss Monks, did you see the witness list?" asked Mike.

"No, sir, why?"

"Your name is on there as a witness for the prosecution."

"Oh, sir, I cannot go into a court-martial; I won't do well on the stand."

"I understand and I will try and help you through this issue."

"Yes, sir."

"All of you, please go back to your quarters and check your dress blue uniforms and return here after you have inspected them. If you're in the court-martial with me, you will have to be wearing that uniform as it is proscribed in this message."

"Yes, sir," everyone said as they left the office.

Mike left the office and went to see the Medical Officer, Captain Cruz. She smiled as Mike entered into the sickbay. He looked around the sickbay and noticed that it was just about empty. He stepped up to her desk and stared down at her.

"Yes, Warrant Officer Weatherspoon, what can I do for you?" she asked.

"I received the list of witnesses for the prosecution. Miss Monks is on that list and she doesn't do well on the stand from what she has told me."

"I understand, Mike. I will have one of my Medical Technicians Level Four give her a mild tranquilizer tomorrow morning."

"Thank you and I appreciate your help."

"Anytime. You've got a tough case for your first assignment."

"Yes, I do, thank you," said Mike as he left her office.

Mike went down and saw the accused. After the door was shut behind him, he looked at the accused who was now standing at attention. Mike carried with him a copy of the list of charges and the list of witnesses and jurors. MA1 Masterson nodded his head up and down indicating that he was satisfied with the jury pool.

"Would you please sign the statement," said Mike.

"Yes, sir," replied MA1 Masterson as he signed it electronically.

"The court-martial will begin tomorrow morning at 0800 hours. Do you want to tell me anything before the court-martial begins?"

"Yes, sir. The person that I am accused of killing was a hermaphrodite."

"I'm glad you told me this information. Now I know why the dead person's best friend was so hostile towards me. Did anyone else know about this oddity?"

"No, sir, I don't think so."

"Is there anything else?"

"No, sir."

"Get some sleep and please be in the proper uniform of the day," said Mike as he pushed the call button.

Mike returned to the office and found it quiet once more. Everyone was looking up at Mike as he walked into the office. He looked around at everyone's faces and could see the tension on them.

"Everyone, please try and be relaxed. Miss Monks, tomorrow morning at 0745 hours, you are to report to the sickbay."

"Yes, sir."

"Mr. Bjork, please follow me to my office so that we can go over this case once again."

"Yes, sir."

"Mr. Fracks, please assemble your notes and present them to me within the hour."

"Yes, sir."

"Mr. Groder, is the evidence that I requested available, yet?"

"Yes, sir. I will personally take it up to Battle Room Six and put it on the evidence table tomorrow morning."

"Thank you."

Mike walked into his office followed by Mr. Bjork. When the door was shut, Mike locked the door. Bjork stood there staring as Mike was seating himself in his chair.

"We're going to get creamed at this court-martial," said Mike.

"Then, why are we going through with it, sir? I mean, shouldn't we accept the plea bargain offered?"

"We can't now, it is too late. My client just admitted to me that the man he shot in the back was a hermaphrodite."

"So, I don't see where that is of any concern, sir. The dead man was from the Baltore System. According to STARCORE records, being a hermaphrodite is not uncommon in that culture. The dead man was a STARCORE citizen or else he could not have joined STARCORE in the first place."

"Don't you see? This oddity is going to be used by the prosecutor to provide the jury and the judge with a strong motive for killing MM2 Kelly. Who is to say that this oddity didn't drive my client over the edge, so to speak?"

"I understand, sir. Still, it is all up to the prosecutor to prove the case, correct, sir?"

"Yes, you're correct about that issue. Were you able to obtain the evidence that I asked for?"

"Yes, sir. I have a copy of the ship's sensor logs. The logs show a life form aboard the USS SEA TIGER that is classified by STARCORE regulation 11C as a '...Dangerous, sapient life form to humans...'"

"What is this dangerous life form?"

"The sensor logs show the life form to be a Kelgork."

"Did you say a Kelgork?"

"Yes, sir."

"A Kelgork shoots an acid-like substance out from its mouth, doesn't it?"

"Yes, sir."

"That acid-like substance would burn human flesh, wouldn't it?"

"Unprotected, yes. But unless the attack occurs at extremely close range, our uniforms will protect us from such an attack. Besides, our boarding parties always wear full body armor, sir."

"But at extremely close range, this acid-like substance could penetrate this body armor, is that correct?"

"Yes, sir. It would leave behind the same type of markings as a laser pistol would on human flesh."

"I think we found a way to rattle the prosecution's case against my client."

"Have you prepared your opening speech yet, sir?" he asked, without hearing what Mike had said.

"Not yet, I'm still coming up with it right now. When you leave, send in Miss Monks."

"Yes, sir."

Bjork unlocked the door and walked out into the office. A few moments later, Miss Monks walked into the office. She stood in front of Mike with her electronic note recorder.

"You asked for me, sir."

"Yes, please get me all the information you can on a Kelgork."

"Yes, sir."

"Dismissed," said Mike.

Mike left the office a short time later. He went to see the accused once again. When the door was shut and locked, Mike turned to face MA1 Masterson.

"How far away were you from MM2 Kelly when your weapon discharged?"

"About one to two meters, sir."

"Thank you, that's all I needed to know. Get some rest."

"I will try, sir."

Mike pushed the button on the wall. A few minutes later, the ensign came along and let Mike out of the cell. Mike returned to the office and found Miss Monks waiting for him. She cleared her throat before trying to deliver the report on a Kelgork. Mike walked into his office and shut the door behind him. He sat down in the chair in front of his desk.

"Read me the report, please," said Mike.

"Not much to report, sir. The only thing I could find was that STARCORE's research facilities conducted tests on the Kelgork, live ones, in a restricted environment. STARCORE found that at distances of less than four meters, their acid-like substance they emitted had enough pressure to penetrate body armor."

"Thank you, that will be all. I might have other questions for you while you're on the stand tomorrow."

"Yes, sir."

"Dismissed."

She left and Mike started thinking about what she had said. He also started thinking about what MA1 Masterson had said. Mike picked up the ballistics report on the weapon. The weapon had discharged a 232.065-Joule charge into the deceased. He then looked at the autopsy pictures showing the burnt back and front of the deceased. As Mike looked closer at the pictures, he noticed that the front burnt flesh contained pieces of flesh, body armor and the deceased's uniform. Mike suddenly had an idea and punched the button for the captain.

"Yes Warrant Officer Weatherspoon, what can I do for you?" asked John.

"I need your permission to test a theory of mine. I will need the use of a laser pistol and ordnance gelatin."

"Permission granted, is there anything else?"

"No, sir, thank you."

Mike terminated the conversation and opened the office door. He looked around and saw no one except Miss Monks. He shook his head up and down and motioned for her to come into the office. Once she was inside the office, he locked the door.

"Miss Monks, I want you to go to the armory and check out your STARCORE issue laser pistol. I then want you to report to the ballistics lab in the science section for an experiment."

"Yes, sir. Do I have permission from the captain to do this experiment?"

"Yes, I just obtained you permission. Now, please be on your way. I will call the ballistics lab."

"Yes, sir."

Miss Monks left the office and went to the armory. The Armory Technician Level One, Anthony Beeber, issued her weapon to her. She put on the holster and then put the weapon into the holster. After this was completed, she walked, nervously, to the Science Officer's office. He looked up and saw whom it was standing in the doorway and took her to the ballistics lab. The ballistics lab technician was already preparing for the experiment. Miss Monks was getting more nervous by the minute.

"Miss Monks, you will notice that there are 10 ordnance gelatin blocks in front of you. I need your initials on each one of them prior to beginning this experiment," said the technician.

"Yes, sir."

She went down the row from the far left to the far right placing her initials on each of the blocks. She then returned to the booth, where the technician had her check her weapon to make sure that it had a full power pack in it. After the technician checked that the power pack was fresh, he turned her to face the first block of ordnance gelatin.

"You will fire one shot into each of these blocks at a proscribed distance. Set your charge at 232.065-Joules and approach the first block of gelatin."

"Yes, sir," she said, setting the weapon on the requested power setting. After this was completed, she reholstered the laser pistol.

"Okay, the first gelatin block is to be shot at a distance of .90 meters. Whenever you're ready, step up to the block and point your laser pistol at the block. When the light turns green above the block, you're at the right distance."

"When do I fire?"

"Whenever you're ready."

She nervously approached the first block of gelatin. She pulled out her laser pistol and pointed it at the gelatin block. She practiced her breathing and when the light turned green above the block, she squeezed the trigger once. The weapon went off and sprayed her with ordnance gelatin. It was in her hair and all in her uniform by the time the testing was completed.

"Thank you, Miss Monks. You can return your laser pistol to the armory."

"Thank you."

She returned her pistol to the armory that evening. After dinner, she wondered what that experiment had been all about. She was still thinking about it when she stepped into the shower. After the shower, she was tired and went to bed.

Meanwhile, Mike had been reviewing the computer data on the ballistics tests he had asked to be conducted. All the pictures showed that at no time did any of the laser bolts penetrate completely through the body and exit. After watching this several more times to prove it, he filed it away.

Upon returning to his cabin, he saw someone moving around in his cabin. He tried to reach for the security call button, but the figure hit his right wrist with a very hard object. It was after Mike turned around that he saw who it was; the deceased's best friend and he was pointing a laser pistol right at Mike. Mike quickly ducked out of the way and the laser pistol went off. Thankfully, the laser bolt hit the opposite bulkhead and set off the security alert. The figure quickly moved out of the cabin and disappeared as the ship's security force arrived.

"Alert! Security Alert! Weapons Discharge, Deck 15, Legal Officer's Quarters! Alert! Security Alert! Weapons Discharge, Deck

15, Legal Officer's Quarters! Ship's Security Force respond," said the announcement.

Within minutes, half a dozen security force personnel had invaded Mike's quarters. He was on the deck and looking towards them when they entered. After silencing the alarm, the ship's Security Officer assisted Mike to his feet.

"Are you alright, sir?" he asked.

"Yes, I'm fine. Sorry about the problem I just caused," said Mike.

"That's okay, that's what we're here for; by any chance, did you see who did this to you?" he asked.

"No, sir, I didn't see who it was," replied Mike, who just realized he had told a lie to another officer.

"You wouldn't be lying to me would you?"

"No, sir. My back was to the weapon's discharge. I heard a noise behind me and I hit the deck, sir."

"Okay, as long as you're alright. But, if you think of anything about this little incident that might help me in my investigation, you let me know, okay?"

"Yes, sir."

"Good night."

After everyone had left his cabin, Mike mentally relaxed and set his alarm for early in the morning. He finally laid his head down on his pillow and closed his eyes. It seemed like he had arrived at the deep sleep point when the alarm clock went off. He rolled his eyes a little bit and sat up in bed. After turning on the lights in his cabin, he shaved and then showered.

Next, he looked at the time and decided he needed to get ready for the court-martial. He donned his dress blue uniform with all the appropriate accoutrements and headed out of his cabin. He went to the wardroom and had breakfast without saying much of anything to anyone. He finished off his second cup of coffee and put his tray up in the scullery. He walked passed several other officers in their dress blue uniforms. As he was exiting the wardroom, he ran into Admiral Robbins.

"Mike, you have a big day today, don't you?" he asked, smiling.

"Yes, sir, Admiral Robbins, I sure do. I would appreciate a prayer, not for me, but for my client."

"I will say a prayer for him and you."

"Thank you, sir. I must be going."

Mike went down to the office first. He summoned his office people together for a last minute battle plan.

"I need a runner to stay here in case I need something; I will need it in a hurry. Who wants that position?" asked Mike.

"I will take it, sir," said Fracks.

"Very well, the rest of you come with me."

They all rode the elevator up to Deck 02. When the elevator doors opened, everyone was quietly seated in the passageway. Mike walked passed the officers and others towards the front of Battle Room Six. The door shut behind them and Mike could see the accused seated at the defense table.

Chapter 5

Mike walked passed the prosecutor and pointed to a row of chairs directly behind him for the office staff to sit. They all took their seats and Mike continued to survey the scene. He looked at LA3 Monks, who was sitting quietly in a chair. Mike walked over to her.

"Good morning, Miss Monks. Did you report to the sickbay like I instructed you?" asked Mike.

"Yes, sir. I was given a five-milligram shot of Topazine. The effects should last the entire day," she responded, slowly and confidently.

"Good."

The evidence was laid out on the three-meter long table and all the necessary recording devices were in their proper areas and ready to start recording the event. Mike was very pleased at the arrangement of the evidence. He turned around and mouthed the words *Very good; I am most impressed* to LA2 Groder. He then turned back around to face the prosecutor.

Captain Manning leaned over and looked Mike right in the eye.

"Still time to call this off," he said.

"No deal."

The court bailiff turned to face the courtroom as a small door opened on the portside of the room. This allowed the jury, which had been chosen by the computer, to file into the courtroom and take their seats.

The jury consisted of six officers, two ensigns, one lieutenant junior grade, one major, one lieutenant colonel and one colonel. There were also six enlisted members, one sergeant, one senior sergeant, one missile technician first class petty officer, one fireman recruit, one dental technician second-class petty officer and one seaman apprentice.

"All rise, this general court-martial is now in session. The Honorable General Richard Kelsing, presiding."

General Kelsing looked around the courtroom before taking his seat.

"You may be seated. Are prosecution and defense attorneys ready with their opening statements?" asked the general.

"We are Your Honor," said Captain Manning.

"Prosecution, please present your opening statement."

"Yes, Your Honor."

Captain Manning walked over to the jury and faced them directly.

"Gentlemen of the jury. The accused, seated at the defense table, is here because he committed a crime. I will tell you that after all the smoke and dust settles from this trial, the accused committed the crime and you, the jury, must find him guilty. Now, the accused has a defense attorney that will throw up official terms like Kelgork among others. In the end, the accused committed the crime of killing one of his own crewmembers in cold blood; thank you."

Captain Manning returned to his seat and sat down in the chair. Chief Warrant Officer Number One Weatherspoon stood up and walked over to the jury box. Mike pulled down on his dress blue uniform to make sure that it was straight and took in a deep breath.

"My client now stands before you because he committed a crime. In fact, my esteemed colleague, Captain Manning, has charged my client with First Degree Murder, Second Degree Murder, Manslaughter, Criminally Negligent Homicide, Reckless Endangerment Resulting in Death, Conduct Unbecoming a

STARCORE Petty Officer and Unlawfully Discharging a Weapon Without Proper Authority or while engaged in target shooting."

Mike took in a deep breath before continuing.

"Now, we have all either been part of a boarding party or completed the training thereof. Experiences in the simulator room showing any 'killed' or 'wounded' personnel are nothing more than computer holograms. They're not real. I will show you, the jury, that my client is not a murderer but a victim of the most awful set of circumstances. Once the evidence is presented, you must find my client not guilty of those charges; thank you."

Mike went to go sit down, when suddenly his right bicep was grabbed and squeezed very hard by Captain Manning. Mike turned and looked at the captain and smiled. He even winked his right eye so that the judge and jury couldn't see what was going on between the two of them. Mike sat down as the captain let go of his right bicep. Mike saw the captain turn around to face YN3 Johnson, who was smiling. Mike looked back at his office staff personnel who were displaying confused looks on their faces over the incident.

"I will now officially read the list of charges against the accused." General Kelsing read the list of charges.

"Your Honor, may Prosecution and Defense Counsels approach the bench?" asked Captain Manning.

"You may approach the bench," responded General Manning.

Mike and Jon approached the bench. Jon spoke first.

"Your Honor, I have had a request from some members of the crew that the court-martial be broadcast throughout the ship. I have no objections unless my colleague does?" asked Jon.

"I don't have any objections, Your Honor. However, in accordance with the STARCORE Court-Martial Manual, I would like to confer with my client."

"So noted."

Mike went to the defense table and spoke quietly with MA1 Masterson. Mike soon returned to the bench.

"Your Honor, my client has no objections."

"Then we shall proceed," said General Kelsing.

Both men walked back to their respective tables. Jon shuffled around some discs on his tabletop while Mike looked around the courtroom. There were suddenly lots of cameras and lots of extra eyes. Mike had a bad feeling about how Jon was acting.

"Is the prosecution ready to call their first witness?" asked General Kelsing.

"The prosecution calls Captain John Powers, Commanding Officer of the USS PERFORMANCE," said Jon.

Captain Powers entered the courtroom and walked up to the witness stand. Once he was in the witness stand, he remained standing while facing the judge. Richard looked at him.

"Do you promise to tell the truth, the whole truth and nothing but the truth, sir?" asked Richard.

"I do, Your Honor," replied John, confidently.

"You may be seated."

"Thank you, Your Honor," said John, sitting down in the chair.

Jon approached the witness stand with one of the many discs that were on his tabletop. He placed the disc into the slot on the left side of the witness stand. The computer projected an image of John on the bulkhead behind him and quickly went through his STARCORE history. When the computer had finished, Jon removed the disc and faced John.

"A most impressive record in STARCORE, Captain Powers," said Jon.

"Thank you, Captain Manning, sir."

"You are the commanding officer of this vessel, is that correct?"

"Yes, sir, I am."

"How long have you been the ship's commanding officer?"

"Since her commissioning in the year 2105, sir."

"Were you also her commanding officer when this incident took place?"

"Yes, sir, I was."

"What was the date of this incident?"

"8 July 2112 at or about 1300 hours."

"When were you made aware of the death of one of your crewmembers?"

"8 July 2112 at or about 1415 hours. The ship's Medical Officer, Captain Cruz, informed me that a crewmember had died while aboard the USS SEA TIGER in the engineering section."

"Did the report say what the cause of death was?"

"Objection, Your Honor, the captain cannot answer that question," said Mike.

"Sustained," said Richard.

"Let me rephrase the question, Your Honor. In the report you received from Captain Cruz, did the report state the cause of death?"

"Yes, sir, the report did state the cause of death."

"No further questions, Your Honor. Your witness," said Jon, as he sat back down at his table.

Mike stood up and walked over to the jury box before walking over to the witness stand. He looked right at Captain Powers and smiled.

"Captain Powers, when was the USS PERFORMANCE scheduled for her next yard period?" asked Mike.

"Her next yard period was scheduled for 1 November 2112."

"That means it was almost four months after the incident, right sir?"

"Yes, sir."

"What were some of the things that were going to be done in this yard period?"

"Objection, Your Honor, irrelevant, immaterial subject matter," said Jon.

"Overruled. Why are you asking the witness this line of questioning?" asked Richard.

"Your Honor, Gentlemen of the jury, I am trying to establish the fact that some upgrades scheduled for the yard period might have been the root cause of the death of this crewmember."

"The witness will answer the question," said Richard.

"The ship was scheduled for engineering upgrades, weapons upgrades and replenishment."

"Thank you, no further questions, Your Honor," said Mike, taking his seat.

"The witness is excused."

John stepped off the witness stand and went outside to the passageway. After the door had shut, the judge looked at the prosecutor.

"You may call your next witness."

"Yes, Your Honor. The prosecution calls Captain Cruz to the stand."

The door opened and the ship's Medical Officer, Captain Rosalinda Cruz, stepped into the courtroom. She walked down the isle and, after entering the witness stand, she looked right at Mike and smiled. She then looked up at the judge and the prosecutor. Jon walked up to the witness stand as the judge read her the same speech.

"Do you promise to tell the truth, the whole truth and nothing but the truth, ma'am?"

"Yes, Your Honor."

Jon placed a different colored disc into the slot. The computer read the disc and displayed her picture and went over her STARCORE medical qualifications. She was not only trained in being a human doctor, but she was also a dental doctor with surgical board certification and one of the few qualified in STARCORE as a veterinarian.

"A most impressive STARCORE Service Record, Captain Cruz," said Jon.

"Thank you, sir. It has taken quite awhile to get to that level, sir," she responded, while looking directly at the jury and then shifting her gaze to the judge and back to the prosecutor.

"Were you the ship's Medical Officer on the date in question?" asked Jon.

"Yes, sir, I was."

"When did you find out about the dead crewmember?"

"I was informed of the death of the crewmember at or about 1400 hours on 8 July 2112, sir," she said, answering the question while facing the jury.

"Did you examine the body?"

"Objection, Your Honor, calls for testimony that the witness does not have first hand knowledge of, sir," said Mike.

"Sustained, please be more careful, Captain Manning," said Richard sternly.

"Yes, Your Honor, I will be more careful. Did you participate in the post mortem examination of the dead crewmember?"

"No, sir, I did not participate in the autopsy as it is properly called in STARCORE."

"I see. What was your participation level in the autopsy?"

"My job was to make sure that pictures of the dead were taken showing the injuries that they suffered. I was also required, by STARCORE Medical Corps Instruction 3344.9R, to fill out STARCORE Form 0100, the Death Certificate."

Mike, during this whole time, had been paying little attention to the prosecutor. Instead, he was looking at the jury and seeing something there in the jury. The jury was responding to her in a unique way; Mike sought to exploit this immediately during cross-examination.

"So, you made sure that the autopsy photos were taken and that the Death Certificate was signed, is that correct?" asked Jon.

"That is correct, sir."

"Your Honor, I would like to show the jury prosecution's evidence mark exhibits R thru Z; the autopsy photos."

"Granted, if defense counsel has no objections?" asked Richard, looking directly at Mike.

"I have no objections, Your Honor," responded Mike.

The pictures were shown to the jury. The charred flesh from both the back and front of the body were shown. Mike took careful mental notes as to what photos he wanted to be shown later. After the photos had been shown to the jury in a slideshow presentation, the room returned to normal.

"Captain Cruz, can you be certain as to the cause of death?" asked Jon.

"Objection, Your Honor, calls for speculation on the part of the witness," said Mike.

"Overruled, the witness will answer the question."

"I would say that the most likely cause of death was a single laser bolt to the back that entered the back between the fifth and sixth Thoracic vertebrae. That explains the charred flesh on the back of the body."

"Did the laser bolt exit the body?"

"I do not think so, even at extremely close range."

"No further questions, Your Honor. Defense's witness," said Jon as he took his seat.

"Captain Cruz, although you do have a very impressive STARCORE Service Record, do you have training as a criminologist?"

"No, sir, I do not have any formal training in that area. My general knowledge of things is what allows me to have a wide variety of personnel working in my department."

"Objection, Your Honor, irrelevant, immaterial," said Jon.

"Your Honor, this line of questioning is very relevant and very material to this case. I am merely showing that, although Captain Cruz, here, signed the death certificate and has many qualifications within the STARCORE Medical Corps, she does not have any formal training nor education in criminology."

"Sustained," said Richard.

"Captain Cruz, what is the normal procedure for you and your medical crew when a law enforcement boarding party is sent to check a ship out?"

"My crew and I are required to comply with STARCORE Instruction 7699.12D, STARCORE Procedures for Boarding Ships During Law Enforcement Operations."

"Please describe, generally, what the procedure is for the medical crew."

"Objection, Your Honor, irrelevant and immaterial question."

"Your Honor, I am trying to show to the jury and this court-martial that policy and procedure was followed."

"Overruled, the witness will answer the question," said Richard.

"Thank you, Your Honor."

"During the boarding of a ship, Paragraph 22 of STARCORE Instruction 7699.12D applies to the medical crew. The medical crew must be located at a point nearest to the boarding party crew, but not close enough that the medical crew does not have adequate protection. This area may be modified by the commanding officer of the ship that is doing the boarding."

"And where does the commanding officer of this vessel designate as your area to set up in?" asked Mike.

"The hangar deck is the normal place, however, on this particular law enforcement boarding, Captain Powers modified the place of staging."

"Modified the place of staging, eh? Had the captain done this before this mission?"

"No, sir, he had not modified the place of staging."

"No further questions, Your Honor," said Mike as he sat back down in his seat.

"The witness is excused. This court-martial will reconvene at 1300 hours today," said Richard, banging his metal gavel down on the tabletop.

Everyone exited the courtroom. Mike stayed behind after MA1 Masterson had been led away by the ship's security force. As the office staff was preparing to leave, Mike held up his hands to stop everyone.

"Assemble in the office after lunch at 1215 hours," said Mike.

After everyone was in the office, Mike walked inside the office and locked the door behind him. Everyone was looking around the office as Mike started pacing around. Finally, Mike stopped and looked at the office members.

"Let's rotate runners. LA1, I want you up in the courtroom with me, taking notes at all times. Not necessarily about what is being said, but how people are reacting," said Mike.

"Yes, sir. Who is going to be the new runner?" he asked.

"LA2 Groder will be in that position. Now, can anyone tell me why the prosecutor asked the judge to broadcast the court case?"

"I can think of only one reason; the prosecutor wants to show you off as a fake or fraud perhaps, sir. He may know that this is your first case," said Monks.

"Good thinking and probably very true. Does anyone know what happened to me last night in my quarters?"

"Yes, sir. The news is all over the ship, someone tried to kill you last night," said Groder.

"Quite right, LA2. Now, why would someone want to kill me?"

"Because you're a threat to them in some manner," said Bjork.

"Again, quite right. Now, who would want me dead?"

"YN3 Johnson, sir," said Fracks.

"What made you arrive at that conclusion, Mr. Fracks?"

"Our run in with him yesterday afternoon, sir. He said something to the effect of, only a coward shoots someone in the back, sir."

"Right again. Now, we have established a motive for trying to kill me, but why?"

"If MA1 Masterson is acquitted of the charges, then YN3 Johnson will not feel any justice has been served and do it himself."

"Exactly. Now, officially, I told the ship's Security Officer that I did not see whom it was who had taken a shot at me. I told him my back was to the person."

"Was it really, sir?" asked Bjork.

"I'll let you debate that later, however, you're quite right in that deduction. Now, let's all go back up to the courtroom."

Everyone filed back into the courtroom. Captain Manning was waiting with his first witness of the next round of witnesses. Mike looked around and saw the ship's security force standing at the back and off to both port and starboard sides of the courtroom. The evidence was still on the tabletop. The bailiff stood at attention when General Kelsing walked into the courtroom.

"All rise, this court-martial is back in session, the Honorable General Richard Kelsing, presiding," he announced.

"You may be seated. Mr. Prosecutor, call your first witness," said Richard.

"The prosecution calls Pathologist Level One, Gary Bussy."

The witness took the stand and Mike watched, as the man was obviously nervous on the stand. Mike knew that this nervousness might be used to the witness' disadvantage and Mike's advantage. Jon walked up to the witness stand and placed another one of the colored discs into the slot. The man's STARCORE Service Record appeared on the screen.

"You are the USS PERFORMANCE's Pathologist Level One, is that correct?" asked Jon.

"Yes, sir, that is correct."

"Did you have the occasion to conduct an autopsy on the deceased on or about the 8th of July, 2112?" asked Jon.

"I did, sir."

"What were your findings?"

"The deceased was dead, sir."

The entire courtroom chuckled a little at that comment.

"Let me rephrase my question. Where you able to determine, during this autopsy, the cause of death?"

"Yes, sir. The deceased had been shot, by a laser bolt from a STARCORE issued Mark VII Laser Pistol, at extremely close range, in the back, between the fifth and sixth Thoracic area of the spine. The spine was severed at that point and the deceased died a short time later in the sickbay," said the man, pointing at one of the autopsy photos of the dead man's back.

"How do you know it was a laser bolt? Did you do a ballistics test on the weapon?"

"The tissue samples that I sent to the science lab aboard this ship proved that the laser bolt came from a STARCORE issued, Mark VII Laser Pistol. No, I didn't do the ballistics test on the weapon."

"Is that weapon present in this courtroom?"

"Yes, sir. The weapon is sitting on the table in front of me."

"Is this the weapon?" said Jon, picking it up and handing it to the man.

"Yes, sir, this is the weapon. As you can see, I marked my initials into the bottom of the laser pistol's power pack with a laser pen," said the man, pointing to the markings.

"Your Honor and gentlemen of the jury, let the records show that the witness identified the weapon marked as exhibit A as the one he examined."

"So noted," said Richard.

"How many times had the deceased been shot in the back? Or did I ask you that question already?" Jon asked as he set the weapon back down on the table.

"Only once, sir. The lab report indicated that the deceased had received a 232.065 Joule charge from the weapon."

"Thank you. You're witness, Mr. Weatherspoon," said Jon as he sat down at the table.

"Mr. Bussy, when did the autopsy take place?"

"At or about 1600 hours on 8 July 2112 after the deceased was declared dead by the ship's Medical Officer Captain Cruz."

"Getting back to your autopsy photos, can you tell me what you found on the front of the deceased's body?"

"I found parts of his body armor, uniform and an unidentifiable substance."

"Did you make an attempt to identify this unidentifiable substance?"

"No, sir, I did not."

"Could a laser bolt at close range penetrate and exit a human or humanoid body?"

"No, sir. I have been doing autopsies for the past six years and so far, even if the body was shot multiple times, the laser bolts never went through."

"Why is that?"

"The human body is very liquid. Laser bolts don't do well in water, sir."

"True. What would you say the distance was from the laser pistol to the body?"

"Objection, Your Honor, calls for speculation on the part of the witness."

"Overruled, the witness will answer the question."

"I would estimate a distance of no more than two meters."

"Thank you, I have no further questions of this witness, Your Honor and wish to present defense exhibits 1 through 10 into the court record."

"If prosecution has no objection?"

"Prosecution has no objections, Your Honor."

"So noted."

"Gentlemen of the jury, Your Honor. Those pieces of ordnance gelatin that are marked 1 through 10 are the results of a carefully engineered experiment. I received permission from the commanding officer to conduct the test and to testify to their authenticity, I have both LA3 Monks and the ballistics scientist who oversaw the experiment."

"Objection, Your Honor, on what grounds is this evidence proving anything?" asked Jon.

"Your Honor, I'm merely trying to show the court and the jury that a laser bolt could not have caused the deceased's death."

"Proceed," said Richard.

"I call Scientist Level Four, Harry Baldwin, to the stand," said Mike.

The man took the witness stand and Mike inserted the man's STARCORE personnel file into the slot on the witness stand. After the jury and the courtroom were shown the man's qualifications, Mike started with his questioning.

"Mr. Baldwin, do you recognize the items on the table in front of you, labeled defense exhibits 1 through 10?"

"Yes, sir. Those items are the ordnance gelatin blocks you requested to be made to exactly match the consistency of a humanoid body. You wanted them for some sort of an experiment that LA3 Monks conducted in my ballistics lab."

"Mr. Baldwin, did you conduct the tests that I asked for with Miss Monks present?"

"Yes, sir, I did."

"And what were the basics of the tests?"

"You had instructed me to set up 10 blocks of ordnance gelatin in my ballistics lab to be fired at with a STARCORE issue laser pistol very similar to the one that is on the table."

"Did I ask for something specific for these tests?"

"Yes, sir. You specifically asked that the laser pistol used by Miss Monks be set at exactly 232.065 Joules for every charge."

"Anything else?"

"Yes, sir. You asked that the pistol be fired into the ordnance gelatin at 10 preselected distances from .90 meters to 2.125 meters."

"And Miss Monks shot into the ordnance gelatin at the prescribed distances?"

"Yes, sir, she did."

"How did you keep the precise distances so accurate?"

"I had programmed the ballistics computer for the distances and the computer measured the distance from the end of the barrel. I told Miss Monks that when the green light came on, to shoot the ordnance gelatin block and move to the next one."

"Let me show the courtroom that, although some of the blocks of ordnance gelatin are severely damaged, none of the laser bolts set at the 232.065 Joule charge exited the gelatin blocks. No further questions, Your Honor."

"Prosecution, do you have any questions for this witness?" asked Richard.

"No, Your Honor. But, I would like to place Miss Monks on the stand."

"The witness is excused."

Mr. Bussy stepped off the witness stand and Miss Monks took the witness stand. The multi-colored disc contained her STARCORE Service Record and a warning that being in a courtroom or a court-martial makes her extremely nervous. Jon was going to have to make this a quick manner of questioning.

"Miss Monks, I will try and make this quick for you because of your extreme anxiety while in a courtroom," said Jon.

"Thank you, sir," she responded, slowly and confidently.

"On the day of this test that you participated in, did you follow the directions that Mr. Weatherspoon gave you?"

"Yes, sir, I did. I was a little nervous at first, but I completed the order."

"Thank you, no further questions of this witness. Your witness," said Jon, sitting down at his table.

"No questions of this witness, Your Honor," replied Mike.

"The witness is excused. This court-martial is to be reconvened tomorrow morning at 0800 hours." Richard banged the metal gavel down on the tabletop.

Everyone filed out of the courtroom. Mike turned around to speak to the office staff before they left.

"Everyone report to the office on the double."

"Yes, sir," they all said.

When everyone was in the office, Mike came into the office and locked the door behind him.

"Mr. Bjork, who's left on the witness list?"

"YN3 Johnson, the Science Officer, and the Security Officer, sir."

"Everyone get some sleep tonight. Miss Monks, you just earned yourself a much higher rating as far as I'm concerned. You handled yourself very well up there on the witness stand. Mr. Groder, please stay after everyone leaves."

"Yes, sir."

After everyone had left, Mike relocked the door. Mike started pacing around the office before coming to a stop. He looked right at LA2 Groder.

"How many people do we have on the defense witness list?" asked Mike.

"The Weapons Officer and Miss Monks. The other two on the list are considered hostile witnesses."

"YN3 Johnson and the Science Officer?"

"Yes, sir."

"Go to bed. I'll see you at the court-martial tomorrow morning."

Mike went to bed, but didn't sleep that well. His mind was in constant motion. Images flashed in and out of his head. Then it dawned on Mike, YN3 Johnson was a madman suffering from some sort of delirium of some kind. Mike woke up and looked at the clock, 0301 hours. Mike went back to sleep after that nightmare was over.

CHAPTER 6

The court-martial convened the next morning. As everyone took their seats, the prosecutor looked over at Mike and smiled. Mike noticed that the number of colored STARCORE Service Record discs had diminished. Mike looked up as the jury came into the courtroom. The bailiff called everyone to attention.

"All rise, this court-martial is now in session. The Honorable General Richard Kelsing, presiding."

"You may be seated. Prosecution, call your first witness," said Richard.

"The prosecution calls the Science Officer for the USS PERFORMANCE to the stand."

"Objection, Your Honor. This witness is potentially hostile towards the defense."

"Potentially hostile in what way?" asked Richard.

"Your Honor, during my preliminary investigation, the Science Officer, here, would not answer, or evaded, my questions."

"Objection sustained. The jury is hereby instructed that defense counsel for the accused has reason to believe that the witness may hold malevolence against the accused."

"Thank you, Your Honor. You are the ship's Science Officer, is that correct?" asked Jon.

"Yes, sir, that is correct."

"Briefly tell the court, here, what happened on the date in question in the Science Department."

"The USS PERFORMANCE was on patrol in the Alpha quadrant, sectors 86 through 89. Commercial freighters heavily travel these sectors, private yachts and commercial space traffic and sometimes smugglers and other people engaged in illegal trade use these routes as well. The USS PERFORMANCE was under instructions from STARCORE to perform Law Enforcement Operations within these sectors."

"What made you pick the USS SEA TIGER, sir?"

"Objection, Your Honor, my esteemed colleague is asking the witness to testify as to why the USS SEA TIGER was chosen," said Mike.

"Sustained."

"Let me rephrase the question, how many other ships were in the area that the USS SEA TIGER was occupying?" asked Jon.

"There were four other ships in the same sector. However, it was the decision of the executive officer of the USS PERFORMANCE, Captain William Laguer, that made the science department start scanning the USS SEA TIGER carefully."

"Did Captain John Powers approve of this selection?"

"Yes, sir, he did concur with the selection."

"Were there any other things about the USS SEA TIGER that prompted the executive officer to choose her over the other ships in the area?"

"Yes, sir. The USS SEA TIGER had made several ports of call in areas that were known to house pirates and other marauders."

"When did you start the scanning of the USS SEA TIGER?"

"At or about 1045 hours on 8 July 2112 to 1405 hours on 8 July 2112."

"How do you know what the timeframes were?"

"Defense counsel requested for a copy of the ship's sensor logs for those timeframes."

"Did you detect anything unusual about the USS SEA TIGER as the USS PERFORMANCE prepared to board the ship?"

"Yes, sir, there was a sapient life form somewhere in the engineering section of the ship. Our ship's sensors were having a difficult time determining what this sapient life form was."

"Did your sensors ever figure out what this sapient life form was?"

"Yes, sir. Our sensors determined, after the boarding party was aboard the USS SEA TIGER, that the sapient life form was, in fact, a Kelgork, sir."

"Did you notify anyone of this life form?"

"Yes, sir, I did. I notified the boarding party officer in charge, Captain William Laguer of the discovery."

"Do you know what steps Captain Laguer took after you notified him of the discovery?"

"No, I do not know what steps he took, sir."

"No further questions, Your Honor."

Mike stood up and walked up to the witness stand. He looked at the ship's Science Officer for a minute before turning around to face the jury and the courtroom. He drew in a deep breath and let it out slowly.

"I'm curious, sir, why did it take the ship's sensors so long to find out that there was a Kelgork aboard?"

"Objection, Your Honor, irrelevant, immaterial," said Jon.

"Overruled. The witness will answer the question."

"It took so long because the ship in question, the USS SEA TIGER, is Kilorian, L Class Freighter with a Datarian propulsion plant. The reactors aboard the USS SEA TIGER greatly interfered with our sensor scans."

"Why? Were the sensors that far out of calibration?"

"I don't know, sir. All I know is that it took some time before the Kelgork was detected."

"By any chance, sir, were the sensors aboard the USS PERFORMANCE due for overhaul during this most recent yard period?"

"Objection, Your Honor, my esteemed colleague is going on a fishing expedition and I don't see where this line of questioning has any relevance to the case," said Jon.

"Overruled. Defense counsel, where is this line of questioning going?" asked Richard.

"Your Honor, my client is accused of killing one of his own crewmembers in cold blood. I'm trying to prove that a combination of events, such as this long period of time in trying to identify a dangerous life form, may have increased the likelihood of an accidental killing of a crewmember."

"The witness will answer the question."

"Yes, sir, the sensors aboard the USS PERFORMANCE were in need of a yard period adjustment."

"Thank you, sir. Just one quick question, sir, are you familiar with STARCORE Regulation 11C?" asked Mike.

"Yes, sir, I am familiar with that particular STARCORE regulation."

"Would you mind telling the court what this regulation consists of?"

"STARCORE Regulation 11C is a regulation that identifies what STARCORE considers non-dangerous, potentially dangerous, dangerous and extremely dangerous life forms."

"Within this regulation, is there a listing of what STARCORE considers extremely dangerous life forms?" asked Mike.

"Yes, sir. Appendix A contains a listing of 391 extremely dangerous life forms from certain bacteria, virus and fungus to sapient life forms that move and breathe."

"Is the Kelgork on that list, sir?" asked Mike.

"Yes, sir. The Kelgork is on that listing as number 184."

"Thank you, sir. I have no further questions of this witness," said Mike as he sat down.

"The witness is excused. Your next witness, Mr. Prosecutor."

"The prosecution calls the ship's Security Officer to the witness stand."

The ship's security officer took the witness stand. After he was sworn in, the prosecution took on the initiative to start going through the ship's sensor logs and the other ship's logs as well. After the fourth time through all of the logs, Mike was tapped on the left shoulder from behind. He turned around to see Miss

Monks making all sorts of strange hand gestures. The judge caught onto this and pounded his gavel.

"Mr. Weatherspoon, is there something wrong?" asked Richard.

"Yes, Your Honor. I would like to request a 10 minute recess while I confer with my Legal Assistant on an urgent matter to this court," answered Mike.

"So be it; this court-martial shall take a 10 minute recess and reconvene at 1100 hours," announced Richard as he slammed his metal gavel down on the tabletop.

"All rise," said the bailiff as the judge exited the courtroom.

Out in the corridor, Miss Monks looked very nervous. Mike approached her and stood in front of her. She was shaking and very nervous, in fact she was almost too nervous to talk to Mike at all.

"Sir, on the engineering in-deck flight recorder, you can see the Kelgork on the screen for a few seconds before the laser pistol goes off," she said, shaking.

"Okay. Did you have your shot today?" asked Mike.

"No, sir. I want to try and handle this problem without the help of drugs, sir."

"Admirable quality, however, if I put you back on the witness stand, the prosecution is going to tear you up. Mr. Groder!" yelled Mike.

"Yes, sir."

"Please take Miss Monks to the sickbay and have her given the shot, please."

"Yes, sir."

"When you get done, return her so that I can put her on the witness stand."

"Yes, sir."

The court-martial reconvened. The ship's Security Officer took the witness stand once again. As the prosecutor took up the questioning, the judge allowed Miss Monks to return to the courtroom. Mr. Groder had returned as well. Mike had no objections to the questions that were asked. When Mike stood up to interrogate the Security Officer, he was trying to bide his time so that the tranquilizer would take full effect.

"Sir, are you familiar with STARCORE Regulation 11C and its Appendix A?" asked Mike.

"Yes, sir."

"Is there any STARCORE instruction that tells me, as the ship's Security Officer, how to deal with a Kelgork?"

"Yes, sir. STARCORE Security Manual, Chapter 99, Section 12, Subsection G titled Dealing with Extremely Dangerous Sapient Life Forms."

"Tell me, sir, is there anywhere in any regulation in STARCORE that tells me how my weapon is to be set for a boarding party?"

"Yes, sir. STARCORE Security Manual, Chapter 32, Section 18, specifically tells anyone who is on the boarding party that their laser pistol needs to be on a stun setting only."

"Would there be any reason why a laser pistol would need to be set on kill, instead?"

"Yes, sir, there are several reasons for a laser pistol to be set on kill instead of stun."

"Would the finding of the Science Officer detecting a Kelgork be a reason?"

"Yes, sir, that would be one of many reasons."

"Did you arrest my client?"

"Yes, sir. After I was told of his weapon discharging by the ship's science officer."

"Did you read him his rights?"

"Yes, sir and he electronically signed STARCORE Form 1212."

"Did you acquire the weapon from him?"

"Yes, sir and filed the Chain of Custody report form that is still electronically attached to the item."

"No further questions, Your Honor."

"The witness is excused."

"The prosecution now calls YN3 Johnson to the witness stand."

YN3 Johnson took the witness stand. The prosecutor had YN3 Johnson sworn in by the judge and then Mike stood up before the questioning began.

"Objection, Your Honor, this witness is hostile to the defense," said Mike.

"Objection noted," said Richard.

"I understand that you and the deceased were close friends?" asked Jon.

"Yes, sir, until the accused murdered them."

"Objection, Your Honor, irrelevant and immaterial question," said Mike.

"Overruled, this court is trying to find a reason why someone died. I will give the prosecutor a little leeway on this line of questioning."

"Your Honor, I must still post my objection to the witness' hostility towards my client," said Mike.

"On what grounds?" asked Richard.

"When myself and LA1 Fracks were looking around inside the deceased's quarters, the witness was hostile towards me and made a statement that 'Only a coward would shoot someone in the back.' Your Honor."

"Your Honor, I will concede that this witness is hostile towards the accused and I will further stipulate that the witness made such a statement," said Jon.

"Is that acceptable, Mr. Weatherspoon?"

"Yes, Your Honor, it is."

"Now, getting back to my original question, you and the deceased were close friends, were you not?" asked Jon.

"Yes, sir, we were until he died."

"When did you first find out about the death of your friend?"

"When the boarding party came back aboard and I saw the accused in handcuffs and leg irons. I asked one of the medical technicians what had happened and they replied, 'A shooting with someone dying.'"

"What did you do then?"

"I secured my station properly, after receiving the USS SEA TIGER's manifest logs from LN3 Bjork. I then went to the sickbay and was only able to be with that person for a short period of time before they stopped breathing and the life support machine could do no more." At this, YN3 Johnson let a single tear fall from his right eye.

Mike caught onto this right away. He scribbled down a note on the electronic note recorder and slid the recorder to LA2 Groder. He took it and left the courtroom and headed for the office. Mike looked at the man and then decided to ask him only a few questions under cross-examination.

"YN3 Johnson, did you know the deceased's background?" asked Mike.

"Yes, I knew that they came from the Baltore system somewhere."

"You keep referring to the deceased as 'they'; why?"

"The deceased was a hermaphrodite, sir."

"One last question, why do you think that my client killed your friend?"

"Because the deceased, myself and MA1 Masterson were in a polygamous relationship with the deceased."

"Objection, Your Honor, the accused's sexual orientation, sexual preference, sexual bodily functioning or polygamous relationships are not on trial here," said Jon.

"Sustained," said Richard.

"No further questions, Your Honor," said Mike, sitting down at his table.

When he sat down at the table, LA2 Groder handed Mike the answer to the question he had asked. Mike read the answer and then looked up at the judge and then at the prosecutor. Mike merely nodded his head up and down as YN3 Johnson walked out of the courtroom. Richard looked down at Mike before speaking.

"Is the defense ready to put on its first witness?" asked Richard.

"No, Your Honor, we are not ready," responded Mike.

"Very well, does the Prosecution have any more witnesses it wishes to call?"

"Yes, Your Honor, the prosecution calls the Executive Officer of the USS PERFORMANCE, Captain William Laguer, to the stand" said Jon.

Captain Laguer walked into the courtroom. He took the witness stand and, after being sworn in by the judge, was seated in the chair. He faced the defense table and took on a stoic look to disguise the fact that he was very nervous.

"Captain Laguer, were you the boarding officer for the boarding party?" asked Jon.

"Yes, sir, I was the senior officer of the boarding party going aboard the USS SEA TIGER," responded Captain Laguer.

"Were you, at anytime, informed that there was, or possibly was, extremely dangerous sapient life forms aboard the ship that you were boarding?"

"Yes, sir. I was informed, via the chain of command, that the ship's sensors had detected what was later identified as a Kelgork."

"At that time, did you take any precautions of any kind?"

"Yes, sir. I told my boarding party, that was headed towards the engineering section, to be extra careful in that area."

"Did you order any of them to change the settings on their laser pistols from stun to kill?"

"Yes, sir, I gave such an order once, I was informed, via the chain of command, that there was an extremely dangerous life form aboard."

"No further questions, Your Honor."

"The witness is excused. Your next witness Captain Manning," said Richard.

Before Captain Manning could speak, Mike stood up from the defense table.

"Your Honor, I would like to recall YN3 Johnson to the stand," said Mike

"Objection, Your Honor, this is irrelevant and immaterial," said Jon.

"Your Honor, if you please. I have some new information about this case that will help shed some light on why my client is on trial," said Mike.

"Overruled, YN3 Johnson will take the stand," said Richard.

YN3 Johnson took the stand and was reminded that he was still under oath. YN3 Johnson looked a little nervous on the stand. Mike capitalized on the situation.

"YN3 Johnson, you, the deceased and MA1 Masterson here were aboard the same transport ship that brought all of you out to the USS PERFORMANCE, isn't that right?" asked Mike.

"Objection, Your Honor, irrelevant and immaterial," said Jon.

"Your Honor, I ask the court's permission for some leeway to prove that the witness had a reason to hate my client," said Mike.

"I will allow this line of questioning," said Richard.

"I will ask the question again of the witness," said Mike.

"Yes, we were all on the same transport ship, sir."

"Your Honor, I would like to enter into evidence the sexual assault committed by the witness. Both the deceased and the accused knew of this sexual assault. MA1 Masterson here was hot on YNSA Johnson's trial."

The courtroom exploded after that. YN3 Johnson leaped out of the witness stand and took away a laser pistol from one of the security personnel. He fired in the general direction of Mike before YN3 Johnson was struck several times by return fire. Once everything had calmed down, Mike turned to see that Miss Monks was sitting upright in her chair. She opened her mouth to speak.

"That was interesting," was all she said.

YN3 Johnson was taken to the sickbay and was pronounced dead on arrival by ship's Medical Officer Captain Cruz. The courtroom was adjourned as the place was cleaned up and everyone was dismissed for the next couple of days. Mike went down into the ship's brig and saw the accused.

"It would have been nice to know about your little triad love affair," said Mike.

"I'm sorry, sir, it slipped my mind. Did you know that YN3 Johnson was going to do that?" asked MA1 Masterson.

"Oh, I had a feeling that he might do it. You see, he was the one who tried to kill me in my quarters a few days ago. He thought I just might find out about what happened."

"I understand, sir."

"Try and get some sleep."

"Yes, sir."

Mike left the brig and went to his own quarters. He ate late in the evening after all the other officers had already eaten. As he sat down at a table in the back of the wardroom, he started taking mental notes as to how he was going to proceed the day after tomorrow with the defense. He was going to call the weapons officer first, then Miss Monks and then Mr. Bjork. As he was leaving the wardroom, he ran into Rear Admiral Lower Half Robbins.

"Well, hello there Mr. Weatherspoon, how are you doing tonight?" asked Admiral Robbins.

"Doing fine, admiral, yourself?" responded Mike.

"Coming up here for a little peace and quiet."

"I see, admiral, I will leave you alone."

"You know, I've been watching this whole trial from the start. In case you didn't notice it, the crew, the judge, the jury, everyone responds to you. That response characteristic that you possess shouldn't be wasted."

"Thank you very much, admiral for the outside observation. I will think about that in the future; good night, admiral," said Mike, as he hastily left the wardroom.

He stepped onto the elevator and went to his quarters. Upon arrival at his quarters, he took off his clothes and stepped into the shower. After his shower, he realized that one of those laser bolts had singed some of his hair. He shook his head and in the morning, before court, he would get the charred hair removed. He finished drying himself off and then went to bed, setting his alarm clock for early in the morning.

CHAPTER 7

The next morning, Mike ate his breakfast in the wardroom and then went to the ship's barbershop for a haircut. After the barber had removed the burnt hair, he returned to his quarters and took a quick shower. After the shower, he dressed into his dress blue uniform and tucked his hair inside the uniform. Stepping out into the passageway, he went to the office first. He found LA1 Fracks inside the office setting it up for the day.

"Good morning, Mr. Fracks. I need you to do a favor for me, please," said Mike.

"Yes, sir, what can I do for you?"

"Would you please go to the armory and check out a piece of body armor and bring it to the courtroom. Tell the Armory Technician down there that the body armor will be returned," said Mike.

"Yes, sir."

Mr. Fracks left and as Mike turned around, he ran into LA3 Monks. Miss Monks was looking better already. Mike smiled and spoke to her in a slow, calm voice.

"Good morning, Miss Monks. I will be putting you on the stand today after the weapons officer. Are you sure that you saw the Kelgork on the in-deck flight recorder?" asked Mike.

"Yes, sir. I saw the Kelgork in the lower left corner of the USS SEA TIGER's Engineering/Engine Room In-Deck Flight Recorder, sir," she said calmly.

"Okay, I just want to make sure that is what you saw. Do you still remember what you read about the Kelgork?"

"Yes, sir."

"Good, let's go up to the courtroom."

Miss Monks and Mike stepped into the elevator together. The elevator stopped many times to pick crewmembers up and drop them off before the elevator arrived at the 02 level of the ship. She and Mike stepped off and started walking down the passageway to the courtroom. They walked into the courtroom and Mike took his seat. The bailiff stood up, as did the rest of the courtroom.

"All rise, this general court-martial is now in session. The Honorable General Richard Kelsing, presiding," he said.

"Be seated. Prosecution, do you have any more witnesses to present before the defense starts putting on their witnesses?" asked Richard.

"Yes, Your Honor, the prosecution calls the members of the boarding party. Would it be possible, Your Honor, to save on the court's time and if my esteemed colleague has no objections, I would like to put all four members of the boarding party, minus the accused, on the witness stand at one time," said Jon.

"Does defense counsel have any objections to the prosecutor's request?" asked Richard.

"Defense counsel has no objections, Your Honor."

"The witnesses will take the stand," said Richard.

After all of the witnesses were sworn in by Richard, the prosecutor started his questioning.

"You all were part of the boarding party for the USS SEA TIGER, is that correct?" asked Jon.

"Yes, sir," they all answered.

"Did any of you, on the day in question, have the opportunity to see what was going on in the engine room of the USS SEA TIGER?"

"Yes, sir, we all watched as the defendant shot the deceased in the back," they all answered.

"No further questions, Your Honor. Your witnesses, Mr. Weatherspoon," said Jon as he took his seat.

Mike stood up, looked down at the evidence table, noting that the piece of body armor was on the table and then he walked over to the evidence table. He picked up the body armor and walked towards the witness stand.

"Do any of you know what this is?" asked Mike, holding the body armor up in front of all of them. Mike noticed that all their heads nodded up and down.

"Yes, sir. That is a Class IV Body Armor used by boarding party personnel who hold the position of boarding party leader," said one of them.

"Really? How many people are typically on this boarding party?" asked Mike, as he turned around to face the jury.

"Usually six, sir. The person in front is the boarding party leader for whatever section of the ship that must be secured prior to the captain coming aboard. The boarding party leader usually wears a full body armor suit," said the one in the middle.

"Who else is on this boarding party?" asked Mike.

"The defendant, who serves as the point man, sir. Then all of us," said the one to the far left.

"Does everyone on the boarding party wear body armor?" asked Mike.

"Yes, sir. However, those of us behind the point man only wear a partial body armor suit," said the one to the far right.

"On the day in question, were there any words exchanged between my client and the deceased?" asked Mike.

Mike could see the boarding party members look at each other very puzzled. The one in the middle spoke up first.

"What kind of words, sir?" he asked.

"Words like, 'I'm going to kill you and make it look like an accident.' Or perhaps, 'I hate you and I'm going to kill you' etc.?" asked Mike.

"No, sir, no words like that. Although, I did hear the deceased yell something back at the defendant who then shot him in the back," said the one on the far right.

"Do you remember what was said?" asked Mike.

"No, sir. The words were not understandable," said the one in the middle.

"Were you aware that you were being recorded?" asked Mike.

"Yes, sir. We were all aware of that fact," said the one on the far left, rather disgustedly.

"No further questions, Your Honor," said Mike, taking his seat.

"The witnesses are excused," said Richard.

As the witnesses were filing out of the courtroom, Richard turned to face the prosecutor.

"Does the prosecution have any more witnesses?" asked Richard.

"No, sir."

"Is the defense counsel ready to present their case?"

"Yes, Your Honor, we are. The defense would like to call, for its first witness, the Weapons Officer of the USS PERFORMANCE," said Mike.

The Weapons Officer took the witness stand. Mike looked over his STARCORE Service Record and found it to be most impressive. Mike was going to have fun with him on the stand. Mike stood up and walked over to the witness stand. He mouthed the words, *Did you bring what I asked you to bring?* The Weapons Officer merely nodded his head up and down.

"Commander, on the date in question, did you issue the boarding party body armor and their laser pistols?" asked Mike.

"Yes, sir, I did."

"Prior to this incident aboard the USS SEA TIGER, were there ever any reports from STARCORE as to the safety of the Mark VII laser pistol?" asked Mike.

"Objection, Your Honor, irrelevant, immaterial," said Jon.

"Overruled. The witness will answer the question," said Richard.

"None from STARCORE, sir, officially, that is. However, myself and two of my Armory Technicians in the armory discovered something one day that scared us very much," said the Weapons Officer.

"Objection, Your Honor, irrelevant, immaterial. Where is the defense going with this line of questioning?" said Jon.

"I ask Your Honor for some leeway to establish that, possibly, STARCORE knew of a serious design flaw with the Mark VII laser pistols," responded Mike.

"And I assume that you can prove this beyond a reasonable doubt?" asked Richard.

"Yes, Your Honor, I certainly can, with this witness and one other," said Mike, confidently.

"Very well, I will allow this line of questioning for the time being. However, I reserve the right to terminate the questioning at anytime," said Richard.

"Yes, Your Honor, I understand," replied Mike.

"The witness will answer the question," said Richard.

"We discovered that the Mark VII laser pistol had some problems with where the settings button was located. During some of our tests that we conducted on the laser pistol range, we discovered that by merely pulling the weapon out of the holster could change the setting. We also discovered something else, too. If you bumped or jarred the weapon, it would go off unintentionally."

"Could something else cause the settings to be changed?" asked Mike.

"Yes, sir. A sudden jarring of the pistol, if it was in the operator's hands. It would change from stun, to kill, to blast, to heat. We discovered that, if someone had the weapon out, such as during a boarding search, and bumped it up against something or someone else, the weapon would not only change the setting it was on, but also unintentionally discharge."

Mike turned around to see the look on the juror's faces. He could see that they were all thinking the same type of thoughts; maybe his client was innocent after all. Mike turned back around to the evidence table and picked up the laser pistol. He opened the bottom of the laser pistol where the power pack assembly was to go.

"Your Honor, with the court's permission, I would like to temporarily excuse this witness to call another to the stand," said Mike.

"The witness is excused for now," said Richard.

"The defense calls LN3 Bjork to the stand," said Mike.

LN3 Bjork entered the witness stand and, after the computer had read his STARCORE Service Record, he was sworn in by Richard.

"LN3 Bjork, did I ask you to do some legal research for me before this court-martial began?" asked Mike.

"Yes, sir, you did," Bjork answered.

"And what was the nature of this research?" asked Mike.

"You asked me, sir, to find three current case law studies on the possible issue of a defective STARCORE issue laser pistol."

"Did you find such cases?"

"Yes, sir, I did."

"With the court's permission, I would like the court to take precedent knowledge of these court cases for the defense," said Mike.

"So noted," said Richard.

"Objection, Your Honor, irrelevant, immaterial. What good is this going to be to the accused's defense?" asked Jon.

"These court cases are very relevant to my client's innocence, Your Honor," said Mike.

"Overruled. The witness will answer the question," said Richard.

"The court cases were 1011 U.S. 998, *STARCORE V. Wainright*, Case Number 1011 U.S. 999, STARCORE et. al V. *SATURN WEAPONS MANUFACTURING COMPANY* and Case Number 11-009 *Roberts et. al V. SATURN WEAPON MANUFACTURING COMPANY, et. al*, sir."

"Objection, Your Honor, what relevance is this to this case?" demanded Jon, standing up.

"Your Honor, those are just a few of the many cases against the Saturn Weapons Manufacturing Company specifically involving either unintentional discharges or settings that were changed on the Mark VII laser pistol," said Mike, turning to face the jury.

"Overruled," said Richard.

"No further questions of this witness, Your Honor," said Mike turning around to face Jon.

"No questions of this witness, Your Honor," stated Jon.

"The witness is excused," said Richard.

"The defense now recalls the Weapons Officer to the witness stand," said Mike.

The weapons officer took his seat in the witness stand. He looked right at Mike.

"As the Weapons Officer of this ship, the USS PERFORMANCE, did you ever communicate with STARCORE your findings on the Mark VII laser pistol?" asked Mike.

"Yes, sir, I did. From the 3rd of April 2112 to the 18th of August of 2112, I sent many technical problem forms to the Saturn Weapons Manufacturing Company. At your request, I have copies of the forms that I submitted, but I also have copies of the responses from Saturn," said the Weapons Officer, handing over the disc.

"I would like this disc entered into evidence as defense exhibit Z, Your Honor," said Mike.

"So noted," said Richard.

"When were the Mark VII laser pistols removed from STARCORE inventories and this ship?" asked Mike.

"The Mark VII laser pistol was replaced by STARCORE orders with the Mark IX laser pistol. STARCORE fleet personnel were required to turn-in the Mark VII's by the end of 2112. The design problems of the Mark VII have been addressed and eliminated on the Mark IX laser pistols," replied the Weapons Officer.

"So, the possibly defective Mark VII laser pistol was issued to my client, is that correct?" asked Mike.

"Yes, sir, that is correct," replied the Weapons Officer.

"Your Honor, with the court's permission I would like to conduct a little experiment," said Mike.

"Go ahead with this experiment," replied Richard.

Mike walked over to the table and picked up the Mark VII laser pistol. He then walked back over to the witness stand and looked at the Weapons Officer.

"May I please have the power pack that I asked you to bring today," said Mike.

"Yes, sir, it is right here," replied the Weapons Officer as he handed the power pack to Mike.

Mike inserted the power pack and activated the pistol. He then turned around to the rest of the courtroom and set the weapon on stun. The blue light became lit and he handed the pistol around the courtroom for everyone to see. The prosecutor, the judge and even the jury verified that the weapon was set on stun.

"Your Honor, as you can see, I have set the weapon on a stun setting. Now, I will simulate a bump or jar by dropping the pistol on the tabletop here. If the setting changes we shall see it immediately," said Mike.

Mike raised the weapon up to the height of only a few centimeters and dropped it on the tabletop. The weapon, without anyone's finger being on the firing mechanism, not only discharged, but the discharge setting had changed from stun to blast. The bolt tore through the bulkhead into the next compartment. Immediately, alarms sounded throughout the ship.

"Alert! Security alert! Weapons discharge, deck 02, Battle Room Six. Alert! Security alert! Weapons discharge, deck 02, Battle Room Six. Ship's security force and damage control parties respond," said the computer.

In moments, the entire courtroom was filled with ship's personnel. Damage Control personnel were putting out the fire in the next compartment over. Ship's security personnel were standing by in case there was another discharge of laser weapons. After the smoke was cleared and the fires put out in the next compartment, the jury was wide-eyed and concerned. Mike disarmed the weapon by removing the power pack assembly and put the weapon back down on the tabletop.

"Your Honor, I have no further questions of this witness. Prosecution, your witness," said Mike, turning to face Jon.

"Thank you, counsel. Sir, did you implement any type of remedial training to prevent these accidental discharges like we just witnessed?" asked Jon.

"No, sir. We conducted tests of the weapon and found that any type of jarring or bumping would change the settings. The only thing we asked the operators to do, was, double-check the settings to make sure that they had not changed," answered the Weapons Officer.

"But you did take some sort of steps to prevent accidental discharges, didn't you?" asked Jon.

"Yes, sir."

"No further questions of this witness," said Jon.

"I have one last question of this witness, Your Honor. How many accidental or unintentional discharges were there aboard this ship from when you discovered the problem and implemented changes to when the pistols were replaced?" asked Mike.

"159, sir. Thankfully, Your Honor and the jury, 111 of them occurred on the laser range."

"Thank you, no further questions, Your Honor," said Mike.

"Very well, the witness is excused. This court-martial will take a 15 minute recess," said Richard as he banged his metal gavel down on the tabletop.

"All rise," said the bailiff.

After Richard had left, most everyone had left the courtroom. Mike turned to Miss Monks and looked at her.

"You do realize that I will be putting you on the witness stand when this break is completed," said Mike.

"Yes, sir and I'm ready," she replied, a little nervously.

"Okay, did you take your medicine today?" asked Mike.

"No, sir. I must face this demon myself without the help of drugs, sir."

"Fair enough. You realize that you may be cross examined by the prosecutor," said Mike.

"Yes, sir. Again I will conquer this demon myself."

"Very well."

The bailiff stood up as the judge entered the courtroom.

"All rise, this general court-martial is now in session, the Honorable General Richard Kelsing, presiding," he said.

"Be seated. Is the defense ready to call its next witness?" asked Richard.

"Yes, sir. The defense calls LA3 Monks to the stand," said Mike.

Miss Monks stood up from her seat directly behind Mike and walked through the gate to the witness stand. After taking the stand and placing her STARCORE Service Record in the appropriate slot, the bailiff swore her into the court-martial. She straightened her uniform a little and took in several deep breaths. Mike approached and smiled at her.

"Miss Monks, did I ask you to do some legal research for me for this case?" asked Mike.

"Yes, sir, you did," she replied slowly.

"And what was that research in reference to?" asked Mike.

"You asked me to find all the information that I could on the Saturn Weapons Manufacturing Company et.al," she said, slowly and confidently.

"And what did you find during your research?" asked Mike.

"The Saturn Weapons Manufacturing Company was in legal trouble over their Mark VII issue laser pistol. It was found, during tests conducted at one of the STARCORE Research and Development Facilities on Saturn's Moon Titan, to be defective," she said, taking many deep breaths before completing the sentence.

"What was the nature of this defectiveness?" asked Mike.

"A bump or jar could unintentionally discharge the weapon. This research and development facility also found that the operator's trigger finger did not have to be on the trigger for this discharge to happen," she said.

"Thank you, no further questions of this witness," said Mike, sitting back down at the defense table.

"Miss Monks, are you scared of courtrooms and trials?" asked Jon as he stood up from behind his table and walked towards her.

"Yes, sir, I am. Courtrooms and court trials make me extremely nervous," she replied, her voice cracking slightly.

"Are you on any drugs at this time?" asked Jon.

"Objection, Your Honor, irrelevant, immaterial," said Mike.

"Sustained. Mr. Prosecutor, where are you going with this line of questioning?' asked Richard.

"I'm trying to prove that the witness here may be under the influence of drugs and her testimony may be clouded," replied Jon.

"That is very interesting. The witness will answer the question," said Richard.

"I am not on any drugs at this time, sir," she replied.

"Okay, then answer this question, under what conditions were these tests conducted?" asked Jon.

"STARCORE required that the tests conducted simulate the weapon being removed from a holster and various other bumping and jarring conditions, sir."

"How many tests were conducted?" asked Jon.

"150, sir."

"And out of those 150 tests, how many discharges occurred?"

"140, sir."

"No further questions, Your Honor," said Jon as he sat back down at his table.

"Miss Monks, did I ask you to do other research for me?" asked Mike standing up again and approaching her.

"Yes, sir, you did," she said taking in long, deep breaths.

"What other research did I ask you to do for me concerning this case?" asked Mike.

"You asked me to do research on a Kelgork, sir," she said, with more confidence.

"And what did you find?" asked Mike.

"Objection, Your Honor, irrelevant, immaterial," said Jon.

"Sustained. Defense counsel, where are you going with this line of questioning?" asked Richard.

"Your Honor and the jury, a Kelgork, although considered an extremely dangerous sapient life form, has a unique defensive weapon which could account for the burns on the front of the body on the deceased. The deceased may have been acting in defense of his other crewmembers when the Kelgork attacked, shoving his now dead body into the defendant here causing his weapon to unintentionally discharge into the deceased's back," said Mike.

"I will allow this line of questioning," said Richard.

"What did your research come up with on the Kelgork?" asked Mike.

"The Kelgork prefers not to confront a larger adversary. If this other adversary is larger or more heavily protected, the Kelgork has a defense mechanism of shooting a large volume stream of an acid-like substance about four meters maximum distance."

"How strong is this acid-like substance?" asked Mike.

"This acid-like substance is strong enough to eat through all known fabrics, humanoid flesh and some metals. The acid-like substance would leave behind a burn pattern, according to the STARCORE files I found on the creature, at the point of impact, that would be very similar to a laser pistol hit," she said.

"Does this acid-like substance have any force behind it?" asked Mike.

"Yes, sir, it does. The force is considerable, especially at one meter or less. The force would be enough to knock someone off balance."

"In other words, someone hit with this defense mechanism could lose their balance and be pushed backwards?" asked Mike.

"Yes, sir, that is entirely possible."

"So, someone could be pushed back into someone standing behind them which might cause the person standing behind them to unintentionally discharge their weapon?"

"Yes, sir, it would be very possible."

"Thank you. I would like to move to the next part of the defense, Your Honor," said Mike.

"After lunch, perhaps. This court-martial will reconvene at 1300 hours," said Richard, banging his gavel down on the tabletop.

"All rise," said the bailiff.

After everyone had left, Mike joined Miss Monks in the mess hall. She looked up at him and smiled a little. Mike put his tray down and started eating, only to be bothered by the cook with his paperwork again on the quality of the food, etc. Mike smiled and agreed that he would take care of the paperwork.

"How are your nerves holding out?" asked Mike.

"I'm holding my own, sir," she replied.

"Good. Because after lunch, I'm going to put you back on the witness stand and you can show everyone the Kelgork you saw," said Mike.

"Do you think that the jury will buy any of what we are doing?" she asked.

"I think the jury and judge both have some doubt as to whether the accused really did, intentionally, kill his own crewmember," replied Mike.

After the lunch break was over, Mike put Miss Monks back up on the witness stand. She drew in a few deep breaths before looking at Mike.

"Miss Monks, did you tell me, a few days ago, when the prosecution was showing us all the in-deck flight recorder of the accused shooting the deceased in the back, that you saw something else on the screen?" asked Mike.

"Objection, Your Honor, the jury does not need to see the killing again," said Jon.

"Sustained. What can be accomplished by showing these flight logs again?" asked Richard.

"Your Honor, Miss Monks told me that she saw the Kelgork on both the USS SEA TIGER's in-deck Engineering/Engine Room Flight Recorder on the portside where the boarding party was entering, but also on the in-deck flight recorder for the portside passageway," said Mike.

"Proceed," said Richard.

"Your Honor and jury personnel, if you look in the lower left hand quadrant of the images, you will see the Kelgork and it appears that this creature is taking up a defensive posture," said Miss Monks.

The computer played the in-deck flight recorders and the entire courtroom was able to see the Kelgork. A faint sound of a hiss could be heard on the recorder, as the deceased moved backwards towards the defendant. This all occurred right before the laser pistol went off. After the courtroom had seen this, the judge turned to the prosecutor.

"Mr. Prosecutor, do you have any questions of this witness?" asked Richard.

"No, Your Honor," replied Jon.

"Your Honor, the defense rests its case," said Mike.

"So noted," replied Richard.

"Your Honor, the Prosecution also rests its case," said Jon.

"So noted. This court-martial will reconvene tomorrow morning at 0800 hours at which time, both parties will present their closing arguments," said Richard, banging his metal gavel down on the tabletop.

Mike went to dinner in the wardroom where all he could overhear in conversations was the court-martial. He didn't really hear too much of the conversations, but enough to hear that he was either going to be hated or revered by the crew after this case was over. After finishing off dinner, Mike returned to his cabin to find his lover inside his cabin.

"It's good to see you Chief Warrant Officer Number One Mike Weatherspoon," said Karl, an Armory Technician Level Two.

"You know that you're not supposed to be in officer's quarters after hours. You could get into trouble," replied Mike.

"I had to take the chance just to see you. Oh, I have missed you since we first met, years ago," said Karl.

"I remember well. Now, you're welcome to stay the night or you can sneak back down to your own quarters."

"I'll stay here tonight and risk it in the morning," said Karl.

Mike turned off his quarter's lights and went to bed.

CHAPTER 8

Mike woke up early the next morning. He woke Karl up and double-checked the passageway to make sure that Karl had not been spotted coming out of Mike's quarters. After Karl left, Mike dressed into his dress blue uniform and went to the wardroom to have breakfast. After breakfast, Mike went to the courtroom and sat down in his seat. MA1 Masterson looked over at Mike with a concerned look on his face. The bailiff stood up, as did everyone else.

"All rise, this general court-martial is now in session. The Honorable General Richard Kelsing, presiding," he said.

"Be seated. Are the prosecution and defense counsels prepared with their closing arguments?" asked Richard.

"Prosecution is ready," said Jon.

"Defense is ready," said Mike.

"The Prosecution may enter their closing arguments," said Richard.

"The accused, sitting before you, killed the deceased on 8 July 2112. The in-deck flight recorders show his laser weapon going off. The accused's fingerprints are on the murder weapon. I ask that you find the accused guilty on all charges, thank you," said Jon.

"Thank you, Mr. Prosecutor. Defense counsel, are you ready?" asked Richard.

"Yes, Your Honor. The jury, Your Honor, you must find the accused not guilty on all charges. I believe that my client was the victim of the most terrible set of circumstances that any humanoid has ever been subjected to. I proved, without my client ever having to take the witness stand, that he did not intentionally discharge his weapon at the deceased and that the deceased, I feel, needs to be decorated for trying to save the lives of his fellow crewmembers. The deceased saw an imminent threat to his fellow crewmembers and used himself as a humanoid shield to protect everyone in the boarding party. The fact that my client's fingerprints are on the murder weapon is of no surprise. The murder weapon was in fact assigned to my client by the Weapons Officer's Armory Technicians for boarding party purposes."

Mike took in a long breath before continuing.

"My client does not dispute the fact that the laser weapon, that was in his hand, did discharge. However, I would like to think that perhaps this will be the final case of the defective STARCORE issue Mark VII laser pistol. We now know that the Mark IX laser pistols are much more improved over the Mark VII's. You, therefore, must find my client not guilty of the charges, or else you find him guilty on all counts; thank you," said Mike sitting down at his table.

"Thank you, Mr. Weatherspoon. The jury, you are to begin deliberation at this moment. You have been supplied, for your convenience, a listing of the requirements of the charges, is such the case?" asked Richard.

"Yes, Your Honor," said the jury foreman, the colonel in the jury pool.

"Begin deliberation at this time, 0945 hours on 9 January 2113. When you, the jury, have reached a verdict, notify the court bailiff of your decision. At that time, this general court-martial is now in recess until the jury delivers their verdict," said Richard, pounding the metal gavel down on the tabletop.

"All rise," said the bailiff, following the jury out the door.

Everyone was speechless on the ship. Mike went and ate lunch in the wardroom. No one else ate lunch with Mike except Rear Admiral Lower Half Robbins. They both ate their lunch in peace and after Mike put up his dishes, he went down to the office. He walked into the office and found it deathly quiet. His office staff looked up at him and he looked back.

"Miss Monks, you did an excellent job at conquering your demon; the courtroom and courtrooms in general. I will recommend a meritorious citation when this case is resolved," said Mike, trying to break the tension in the office.

"Thank you, sir," she said.

"Mr. Bjork, you will make a fine lawyer one day, either as a ship's Legal Officer, or in your own private practice. I suggest that you find out from the Educational Services Office what the requirements are for the STARCORE Legal Corps Academy entrance. I will be happy to sign any forms and type up any letters of recommendation that you may need," he said.

"Thank you, sir. I will get started on that package right away," replied Mr. Bjork.

"Mr. Groder, I think that I can use you to assist Miss Monks on trial preparation paperwork. I think you two will do just fine as a team."

"Thank you, sir. May I say that I reviewed all the notes that I took and you, sir, made everyone respond to you," he replied.

"Thank you, and you're not the only one to have made that same observation; Rear Admiral Lower Half Robbins came to the same conclusion."

"I see," replied Mr. Groder.

"Mr. Fracks, thank you for being there during the questioning of those people in the preliminary investigation stage. I hope that you learned a valuable lesson."

"Yes, sir. I am not to judge someone by their looks or what they say when they answer a question as long as I take into account how they answer the question, sir," replied Fracks.

"Quite correct. Is there anything urgent today?" asked Mike.

"No, sir. However, new crewmember orientation starts tomorrow morning in the hangar deck," said Mr. Bjork.

"I see. Would one of you volunteer to stay down here in the office and notify me when the jury has reached their decision? The rest of you can have the day off," said Mike.

"I'll stay here, sir," said Miss Monks.

Mike left the office, as did everyone else except Miss Monks. Mike went to his cabin and hung up his dress blue uniform. He laid down on his bed and turned the cabin lights off. He dozed off and woke up in the early evening. He rubbed his eyes and looked at the clock, 1845 hours. He put his dress blue uniform back on and went down to the office. He found Miss Monks doing research on the computer.

"Any word, yet?" asked Mike.

"No, sir. No one has told me anything, yet. Shall I stay any later?" she asked.

"No, that won't be necessary. Go ahead and close up the office and get something to eat."

"Yes, sir."

Mike watched her as she locked up the office. After he watched her walk down the passageway towards the elevator, he took the time to wander around the ship. He found Damage Control Central, the Engine Room, the Reactor Room. He continued wandering about the ship and found the Computer Room and Computer Core, he found the Weapons Control Room and then he made his way, finally, to the bridge. Stepping off the elevator onto the bridge, he was noticed only by the Officer of the Deck, the ship's Weapons Officer.

"Is there something I can do for you, Warrant Officer Weatherspoon?" asked the Weapons Officer.

"No, sir. I was just looking around the ship. I suppose I will see you at tomorrow morning's crewmember orientation, is that correct?" asked Mike.

"That is correct, sir. By the way, I believe that your client will be found innocent of the charges against him," said the Weapons Officer with a smile and a curt nod of his head up and down.

"Thank you, sir. I think I will go to bed right now," said Mike, yawning.

Mike left the bridge and went to his quarters. He set the alarm and when the alarm went off, he stepped out of bed. He turned the computer monitor screen around so that he could see it better, he found out what the uniform of the day was going to be and put that uniform on. After breakfast, he went to the hangar deck and joined everyone else in the new crewmember orientation. By the end of that day, the jury still hadn't reached a verdict. Mike went to bed that evening and set his alarm clock.

He went back to new crewmember orientation and, this time, there were several officers present. Each officer went over what they were responsible for and then they turned everything over to the ship's Command Master-Chief Petty Officer Miss Frye. Miss Frye let the new crewmembers introduce themselves to each other and then she took them all on a short tour to show them where everything was at aboard the USS PERFORMANCE. When everyone had returned after lunch, Miss Frye had Mike stand up and explain whom he was and what some of his duties were.

"Thank you, Miss Frye. I'm Mike Weatherspoon. I graduated from STARCORE Legal Corps Academy this year with high marks," he started, when one of the new crewmembers interrupted him.

"How much law training do you have, sir?" she asked.

"I have law training from the Code of Hammurabi to the U.S. Constitution to the Martian Laws and beyond. I have general training in almost all forms of criminal justice," replied Mike, confidently.

"What are some of your duties here aboard this ship?" asked Miss Frye.

"I am here to process all legal documents, legal requests and I can sign for search and seizure warrants if necessary and I can witness, sign and approve certain legal issues," replied Mike.

One of the crewmembers raised his right hand.

"Yes, Damage Controlman Zephyr?" asked Miss Frye.

"What are your hours, sir?" he asked nervously.

"I am available 24 hours a day, 7 days a week," answered Mike.

"Thank you, sir. How are you handling this time the jury has taken in its deliberation?" he asked.

"I'm doing quite well. However, my client may not be doing as well."

As the day progressed to an end, Mike checked on the status of the jury. He stopped by the office and looked in on who was there. This time he found LA1 Fracks in the office and no one else.

"Any word?" asked Mike.

"No, sir. Still no word from the judge or the jury, sir," he replied.

"I sense that you're worried, Mr. Fracks," said Mike.

"Yes, sir."

"Let me tell you something about juries. The longer they take to reach a decision, the more likely they are to find your client not guilty."

"Thank you, I will take that under advisement."

"Good night," said Mike as he walked out the office.

Mike went to bed and stepped out of bed the next morning. He ate breakfast in the wardroom and noticed that no one wanted to sit with him. He decided thereafter, not to eat in the wardroom, but in the mess hall where at least people would talk to him. Mike went back to the hangar deck and was told to follow the other officers.

All new officers had to go through training aboard the USS PERFORMANCE. This training consisted of practical damage control skills, basic fire fighting procedures, security training, weapons and body armor issue and, finally, training on how to be the underway Officer of the Deck or the in-port Command Duty Officer. When he had finished off his tests and was considered qualified for the ship's security force position, he stepped out of the wardroom with the other officers and was greeted by Miss Monks. She saluted and he returned the salute.

"Sir, the court-martial has reconvened. Your presence is requested in Battle Room Six, sir," she said, as calmly as she could.

"Lead the way," he replied.

He followed her up to the courtroom and walked inside. The door shut behind them both and he sat down next to his client. The bailiff stood up, as did everyone else. The jury filed in and took their seats.

"All rise. This general court-martial is now in session. The Honorable General Richard Kelsing, presiding," he said, dryly.

"Be seated. Has the jury reached a verdict in this general court-martial?" asked Richard.

"We have, Your Honor," said the jury foreman.

"Will the bailiff please hand me the jury's verdict," said Richard.

The bailiff walked over to the jury foreman and retrieved the black disc. The bailiff handed the black disc to Richard who inserted it into the reader. He looked up at both the prosecution and defense. He looked over the verdict and then cleared his throat.

"Will the accused please rise?" asked Richard.

Mike and MA1 Masterson both stood up.

"We the jury find the accused not guilty on the charge of First Degree Murder. On the charge of Second Degree Murder, we find the accused not guilty. On the charge of Manslaughter, we find the accused not guilty. On the charge of Criminally Negligent Homicide, we find the accused not guilty. On the charge of Reckless Endangerment Resulting in a Death, we find the accused not guilty. On the charge of Conduct Unbecoming a STARCORE Petty Officer, we find the accused not guilty. On the charge of Unlawfully Discharging a Weapon While not Engaged in Target Practice at an Authorized Laser Pistol Range, we find the accused guilty."

Mike grabbed MA1 Masterson by his right arm.

"Don't panic yet, that charge is a misdemeanor with a light sentence," said Mike quietly.

"It is the finding of this general court-martial that the accused is guilty of the crime of Unlawfully Discharging a Weapon While not Engaged in Target Practice at an Authorized Laser Pistol Range. Due to the fact that this court is aware that the accused was in the ship's brig for approximately 190 days before he was afforded legal counsel, the court finds that the accused has time served on his sentence and that in 60 days time, from this date, the charge will no longer be on his STARCORE Service Record. This court-martial is adjourned," said Richard, banging his metal gavel down on the tabletop.

"Mr. Weatherspoon, I appreciate everything you did for me. If you ever go on a landing mission, I would be honored to serve as your guard, sir," said MA1 Masterson, saluting Warrant Officer Weatherspoon.

"I will keep that in mind, MA1 Masterson," replied Mike, returning the salute.

The courtroom cleared out and both the judge and the prosecutor personally thanked the jurors for being on the jury panel. Mike went up to them afterwards with MA1 Masterson and thanked them as well. They told Mike and MA1 Masterson that it was tough, after seeing some of the evidence presented, to convict on the most serious of the charges. Mike nodded his head in understanding and after everyone had left the courtroom, Mike went down to the office.

"I understand now, sir, what being a good defense attorney is really about," said Mr. Bjork.

"I hope that all of you have found this to be a learning experience," said Mike.

"We have, sir. I would be proud to serve on any mission with you," said Mr. Fracks.

"I'll keep that in mind. Everyone get some sleep and I will see you in the morning," said Mike.

Mike went to the wardroom and ate dinner for his last time. As he put his tray into the scullery line to be washed, the scullery attendant looked up at him and smiled. He smiled back and then went to the bridge to shadow the Officer of the Deck for his training.

From 2000-2400 hours every night for the next few weeks, Mike was training to become the underway Officer of the Deck in case someone were to fall ill or not show up for duty. After the final sign-off from the captain, the captain told him not to destroy his ship with experiments gone awry. Mike agreed and soon thereafter, the USS PERFORMANCE was entering the outer limits of NGC-7628 for their star-charting mission. Mike was told by the Executive Officer that he might become part of the intelligence team.

Mike started studying, in his off time, about what the intelligence team did aboard the USS PERFORMANCE. He took proficiency tests and was on the bridge the minute that the USS

PERFORMANCE penetrated the heavy ionized barrier into the solar system that was NGC-7628. Mike went to sleep early that night not realizing that he would be called to serve as the Officer of the Deck because the Educational Services Officer had fallen ill.

Mike reported for duty in the prescribed uniform of the day as ordered by the Commanding Officer. He took over command and walked around to each station to see what was going on. Each station was doing something different for their particular section. Some crewmembers were happy to let Mike see what they were doing, others were a little more hostile about letting Mike see what they were doing.

"Science Section, Bridge," said the Duty Science Officer.

"Bridge, aye," responded Mike.

"Yes, sir. I have completed the initial readings and would like to send the preliminary report to your station for review, sir," she said.

"Very well, send the report to my station," replied Mike.

A few seconds later the preliminary report appeared on the bridge giving Mike the chance to see how many planets, moons, asteroid fields and other items of interest there were in this solar system. As Mike read through the report, he was totally unaware of being observed from one of the possibly inhabited planets.

The ship's Electronic Counter-Warfare Technicians detected the sensor type wave. It hit the ship several times before the computer isolated the frequency range to the range of 900 MHZ to 30 GHZ. The duty ECW Technician called Combat first.

"ECW, Combat," he said.

"Combat, aye," replied the duty combat officer.

"We were just scanned several times, sir. Recommend activating the navigational deflector shield, sir."

"Combat, aye. Combat, bridge,"

"Bridge, aye," replied Mike.

"ECW reports being scanned by something several times. Recommend activation of the navigational deflector shield, sir."

"Bridge, aye. Helmsman, activate the navigational deflector shield and set a course for that green moon on full cruising engines," said Mike.

"Aye, sir."

"Duty Yeoman, go wake up the CO, XO, Science Officer and the Combat Officer," said Mike.

"Yes, sir."

CHAPTER 9

Mike was surprised at how fast the ship reacted to the news of possible, intelligent life in this galaxy. Mike obtained all the information he could about the scanning that had been detected by the ship's Electronic Counter-Warfare section of Combat. The captain, the XO, the Science Officer and others were starting to arrive on the bridge as Mike received the last of the information.

"Captain on the bridge!" yelled the duty yeoman.

"Carry-on," replied Captain Powers.

"Are you relieving me, sir, of the duties of the Officer of the Deck?" asked Mike.

"Not until I find out why you woke us all up at 0202 hours," replied John, squinting at the bridge clock.

"I will brief you immediately, sir. Might I suggest Battle Room One for the briefing?" Mike suggested.

"Very well," replied John as he made his way to the battle room.

Upon arrival at the battle room, the ship was already waking up. Mike filed into Battle Room One and an image of the moon that the ship was hiding behind was present in the room. Everyone took his or her seats around the long, oblong, stainless steel table.

"Okay, tell me why the ship's Legal Officer is the Officer of the Deck?" asked John, trying to wake up more.

"The scheduled Officer of the Deck fell ill before his shift. I understand that he is being treated in the sickbay," replied Mike.

"Well, I hope he gets better. What is going on?" asked John.

"Approximately 40 minutes ago, this ship was scanned by someone, or something, several times," Mike began.

"What defensive measures did you take upon being notified of this scan?" asked the Executive Officer Captain William Laguer.

"This ship was not attacked, sir, merely scanned several times. I didn't think that defensive measures, such as going to battle stations, would be advisable, especially at this hour of the morning, sir," replied Mike.

Everyone at the table started chuckling. Mike was at a total loss to figure out why.

"What's so funny?" asked Mike.

"You answered the question just like it was asked, Chief Warrant Officer Weatherspoon," said John.

"Sorry, sir. I didn't know how else to answer the question, sir," replied Mike.

"Let me ask you this question. What measures, either defensive or offensive, did you take upon being notified of this scan?" asked John.

"I had the helmsman activate the navigational deflector shield and I ordered an immediate course change at full cruising engines to hide the ship behind this moon, sir," replied Mike.

"Very good, warrant officer. Combat Officer, can you tell me more about these scans?" asked John.

"Yes, sir. ECW has sensor logs of four, confirmed, scanning hits, sir," said the Combat Officer.

"Do we know the frequency of the scans?" asked the XO.

"Yes, XO. The scans were rotating, cone-shaped, frequency varying outputs from 900 Megahertz to 30 Gigahertz. The computer confirmed the frequency range belonging to RADAR, sir," replied the Combat Officer.

"RADAR? You mean to tell me someone or something has RADAR in this solar system?" stated the XO.

"Yes, XO, someone or something in this solar system does have at least RADAR capabilities. I would suggest, captain, that we notify STARCORE immediately, sir," said the Combat Officer.

"I will take care of that after this meeting. However, Science Officer, what do we know of this solar system so far?" asked John.

"Very little at this point. We have been making star charts, sir. This solar system appears to be an elliptical type one, which is very rare in our own star system. There appears to be eight planets, 30 moons, seven asteroid fields and other miscellaneous celestial bodies," replied the Science Officer.

"Thank you, Science Officer. Combat Officer, do the ECW logs show the trajectory path of the scans?" asked the XO.

"Yes, XO. The scans originated in the northern hemisphere of the fourth planet from the sun, sir," replied the Combat Officer.

"Are there any other planets or moons that are habitable?" asked John.

"Yes, sir. Planets four, five and six are habitable. All the moons orbiting those planets are habitable, sir," replied the Science Officer.

"Where are we at currently?" asked the XO.

"We are currently on an elliptical orbit around the equator of this moon which is orbiting the sixth planet in this star system. The moon is Class B in nature with jungle like growth all over the surface except in the extreme northern and southern latitudes, sir," replied Mike.

"Very well. Opinions anyone," said John.

"I propose we contact STARCORE and ask for instructions, sir," said the Science Officer.

"I told you, I would take care of that issue after this meeting. Anybody else?" asked John.

"I might suggest, sir, we moon hop all the way to the fourth planet and observe it, sir," said Mike.

"Why moon hop, warrant?" asked the Science Officer.

"Because of the fact that although we can hide from RADAR with the navigational deflector shield, if anyone or anything on that planet has a telescopic type device for looking at the stars, they will see us, sir," replied Mike.

"Very logical, warrant, can't argue with that analogy," replied the Science Officer.

"Perhaps we could send probes to the fourth, fifth and sixth planets," suggested the Combat Officer.

"We could do that, captain. I do have a complete compliment of them," replied the Science Officer.

"Okay, send the probes for now," said John.

"Yes, sir, I will prepare them right now," said the Science Officer as he left the room.

"Officer of the Deck, I am relieving you of your duties at this time," said John.

"Confirmed, sir. I will try and get some sleep," replied Mike.

"Thank you, Mike, for your valuable input and quick thinking," said the XO.

"Thank you, sir."

Mike left the room and went to his quarters. He found Karl in his bed already sound asleep. Mike took off his uniform and hung it up in the closet in his quarters. He then crawled into bed with Karl and fell asleep.

Meanwhile on the surface of the fourth planet, a confused scanning operator was looking at the grainy images of the USS PERFORMANCE taken before she "disappeared" when the navigational deflector shield was activated. The images were shown to the military commander. He looked at the images and picked up the receiver of a communications device. The person at the other end spoke first, in a language that hasn't been spoken on Earth in centuries.

"What do you have?" asked the voice sternly.

"Images of something that I don't think is an asteroid, comet, or meteor," replied the person.

"Bring these images to me and speak to no one," replied the voice.

"Yes, sir," replied the man.

The man took the images to the person at the other end of the communications device and showed them to him. The man looked over the images of the USS PERFORMANCE and then set them down on the tabletop. He then looked up at the man in front of him.

"Did you speak to anyone about these images?" asked the man.

"No, sir," replied the man.

"Does anyone else know about these images?"

"No one that I know of, sir. Of course, the mass communications personnel might have knowledge of it, sir," replied the man.

"Very good. It appears that maybe our ancestors have returned for another visit," said the man.

"This may be true, but these images are not of the best quality."

"This is true. I will see if some reward can be given for better pictures of this thing; dismissed," said the person.

"Yes, sir."

The man departed and returned to his post. He told no one about the contents of the conversation that he just completed. As he sat down at his post, he looked over all the other images. Some of the images were of asteroids, stars, comets and other celestial items. He looked through the windows at his post out to the wide-open area. There, standing stark and tall was a rocket with other attachments to the rocket.

Meanwhile, on the same planet in the southern hemisphere near the planet's equator, an adolescent child was looking through a device he had constructed of pieces of rounded, ground glass that would magnify an image. He had several of these rounded, glass fragments that he had carefully placed inside a piece of metal piping that his father had brought home to him from the place where he worked. The kid thanked his father for the gift and was watching, with some great interest, this mysterious object in the far away reaches of the nighttime sky. The object was moving from one moon to the next in rapid succession. He watched this object moving until he was too tired to hold his eyes open anymore and went to bed.

Meanwhile, aboard the USS PERFORMANCE, the first images of the sixth planet were being processed. The images showed a Class F type planet, habitable with the use of water coaxers and other water gathering equipment. Weather patterns were considered dry and arid with an occasional thunderstorm. The next set of images showed humanoid creatures. The Science Officer determined, by their facial features, that they were descendants of perhaps the Mayans or Toltecs.

More and more images arrived to the ship showing the architecture of the buildings that they lived inside. The buildings had the exterior features of the temples on Earth that the Toltecs and the Mayans inhabited before some unseen force mysteriously eliminated them. As the images were circulated aboard the USS PERFORMANCE, Mike carried out his day-to-day duties as the ship's Legal Officer.

Meanwhile, the probes were touching down on the surface of the fifth planet. The images that were sent back to the USS PERFORMANCE were just as mystifying as the images from the sixth planet. This continued for days and days. As the USS PERFORMANCE crept closer and closer to the fourth planet, the fourth planet prepared itself for an attack. On the dawn of 1 May 2113, the USS PERFORMANCE could hide no longer and was visible for several hours going between moons. As the ship cruised across the stars, the kid again observed it. He was watching more intently this time, as the news of the possible return of their ancestors loomed ever nearer.

During the trip across the stars to the next set of moons, the defense minister for the fourth planet called together his military forces to deal with this problem of the mysterious object in the heavens. The public was demanding protection from another possible relocation by their ancestors and the defense minister was calling on his forces.

All the field generals and naval type personnel were present at this meeting. The images were circulated around the meeting and a decision was made to meet the object with the newly built rocket. A group of volunteers were needed and so a call was put out to all who wanted to meet the object could join. Much against the wishes of the father and mother, the kid joined the defense forces for the planet.

It wasn't until the afternoon of 5 June 2113 that the USS PERFORMANCE picked up the first signs of truly intelligent life. The scans were becoming more intense in their numbers and that's when the communications department detected the radiotelephone type transmissions. The duty person detected the low bandwidth frequencies and started listening in and recording what was said.

"Communications, Science Section," said the duty operator.

"Science Section, aye," replied the duty science officer.

"I'm picking up transmissions in the low bandwidth area."

"We concur."

"What do you show?"

"Pollution, light to heavy industry and some sort of military force. Obviously they might also have some sort of communications system of some kind."

"Do you show any type of radio telescopes and the likes?"

"No, no radio telescopes, but they do have the capacity to make telescopes and perhaps even telephones."

"That might account for the radiotelephone type signals that I am monitoring."

"What are they saying?"

"I'm not sure, I can't make out what is being said. However, I do have the computer linguistics bank working on it."

"Well, I'll add this to my report; good night," said the man.

"Good night,"

Meanwhile, the USS PERFORMANCE was being seen as more of a threat than ever. Newspapers and other mass media were hailing the end of the planet. The public was even more up in arms and the defense minister feared for his life as lawlessness was bound to ensue. The greatest attempts to keep quiet the possibility of their ancestors returning were turning against them. In a last desperate act of saving face with the general public, the defense minister manned and launched the rocket. This was detected aboard the USS PERFORMANCE.

"Combat, Bridge," said the Combat Officer.

"Bridge, aye," replied the captain.

"I have just detected a missile or rocket launch. Solid and liquid fuel propulsion on a direct intercept trajectory course."

"Manned or unmanned?"

"Appears to be manned, sir."

"How many persons aboard?"

"14 total, sir."

"Keep an eye on them and let me know what they do,"

"Yes, sir."

After 20 harrowing moments of flight, the crew, already sick and throwing up all over the place because they were not trained for space flight, prepared their weapons for a boarding of the USS PERFORMANCE. As they approached the object, they were throwing up even more. Now, fatigued by the space flight, the commanding officer ordered his crew to fight this object.

"Combat, Bridge," said the Combat Officer.

"Bridge, aye," said John.

"Sir, I detect that this space vehicle is in trouble,"

"In what way?"

"Sir, I detect extreme stress on the humanoid forms aboard. In fact, I would say that they are in a state of medical emergency."

"Understood. Engineering, Bridge," said John.

"Engineering, aye," replied the Chief Engineer.

"Activate the tractor beam. Very gently bring that space vehicle aboard. Try not to destroy it if you can," said John.

"I'll do my best, sir," replied the Chief Engineer.

The tractor beam brought the small craft aboard. The crew inside was waiting at the door of the small craft and armed. Their weapons were crude, automatic type weapons capable of firing metal projectiles. The captain called away a medical emergency in the hangar deck and a security alert. All personnel involved responded like they were taught. As the ship's Legal Officer arrived in the hangar deck to be back-up security to the ship's security force, the door to the small craft opened and the muzzles swung outwards.

The security force looked at the still vomiting passengers and the ship's Security Officer informed the medical crew that the passengers were indeed having a medical emergency. Everyone was speaking, but no one could understand what was being said. The passengers were escorted or taken by stretcher to the ship's sickbay and kept there until further notice. They received treatment for their space sickness while the Science Officer went over the small craft with a fine-toothed comb. When his inspection was completed, Mike took a look into the sickbay area to see how they were doing.

Captain Powers was receiving reports from STARCORE that said STARCORE didn't want any type of interference on their part. The USS PERFORMANCE was to assist with the medical emergency and get them back to the planet's surface. Mike walked passed the images being displayed on the ship's various bulkheads and noticed something familiar with the architecture. He said nothing of his discovery and, instead, used the ship's computer to look at some ancient cities on Earth. Mike found a striking resemblance between those on Earth five to seven centuries ago and these that were on the planet's surface now.

Meanwhile, Captain Powers was holding an update conference in Battle Room Six. He made sure that all officers knew of the meeting. Mike decided to attend the meeting and put in his thoughts on the matter. He took his seat and the various departments listed their views on the intelligence gathered on these people. It was images that caught Mike's eye more than anything. He was looking at one image of a large compound with two large, tall, fences around the outside and smiled. Captain Powers noticed this.

"Warrant Officer Weatherspoon, do you have something to say?" asked John.

"Yes, sir, I believe that the last images that we looked at were a prison of some sort. It is logical to infer, then, sir, that this culture has some sort of criminal justice system, sir," said Mike.

"So noted. Combat Officer, what about their defenses?" asked John.

"They do have light to heavy industrialization. There is some evidence that they do have at least small arms, automatic weapons, RADAR capacities and even rudimentary space flight capacities, sir," replied the Combat Officer.

"I will put this information into my update report to STARCORE. Is there anything else?" asked John.

"Yes, sir. What do you want me to do with those sick space flight personnel?" asked the Medical Officer.

"Make sure that they make a full recovery," said John.

"Yes, sir."

The meeting was adjourned and Mike went back to his quarters and looked over other images of the cities that the probe had gone through in the night when no one was around. Mike found one image in particular most intriguing. As he had the computer zoom in on the image, he noticed that the building was large, white and had a marble like exterior appearance. He soon became tired and then went to bed.

The next morning, Mike went down to the sickbay and one of the passengers noticed his balanced scales with the quill crossed through it. He looked young, Mike guessed in his teens, and was staring fixated at his balanced scales emblem on his tunic. The young man started bowing to Mike and started speaking that strange tongue the computer couldn't identify. Mike stared back at the young man and then turned around and walked off.

Later that day, during lunch, Mike looked at the images once again of all the planets and their various structures. Mike was more convinced than ever that the structure he had seen was a prison of some kind. As Mike looked over the other images, he noticed something else. Some of those structures were found on Earth. He went looking through the ship's library and found out where those structures were from.

The ship's computer had identified the structures as belonging to the Aztecs, the Toltecs and the Mayans. Mike looked over their various histories and found one common thread between them all. All those civilizations on Earth all vanished without a trace in the matter of one night. Mike started to realize what had happened to them. Some advanced culture had taken them from Earth and placed them on these planets to continue their existence as if nothing had happened. Mike turned to the images of the fifth planet and nothing there made sense.

Mike went back to another officers meeting and took his seat. After everyone gave their reports, Mike raised his left hand. John looked up and acknowledged his left hand being raised.

"Yes, Warrant Officer Weatherspoon, what is it?" asked John.

"Sir, when I was in the sickbay this morning looking after our guests, one of them recognized me; not as a person, but by my emblem on my tunic," said Mike.

"Go ahead, Mike," encouraged the captain.

"I was looking through the images that had been sent back. I then had the ship's computer crosscheck those images with structures throughout the known galaxy of STARCORE. The computer identified, by at least an 88% probability, that the structures on the planet's surface and the ones on Earth are the same," said Mike.

"The same? In what way, warrant officer?" asked the Science Officer.

"Those structures belong to the Aztecs, the Toltecs and the Mayans. The other images, from the fifth planet, seem to indicate a lifestyle of Quakerism dating from the 1600's on Earth in the original colonies," said Mike.

"What are you trying to tell us, warrant officer?" asked the Science Officer, rather disgustedly.

"I think that who we have down in the sickbay are Toltecs, Mayans or Aztecs. I also think that there is a possibility that may be the reason why the computer has had such trouble trying to decipher the language, sir."

"How do you think these people got here?" asked the XO.

"I don't know, yet. I surmise that there is the possibility that an advanced culture came to Earth and took them on their journey across the stars. This advanced culture then deposited these people here to live out their lives."

"What other evidence do you have to support this theory of yours?" asked the captain.

"The Toltecs, the Aztecs, the Mayans and the first colony in the United States all had one thing in common. They all vanished without a trace and their fate is still unknown to this very day," Mike said, looking around the table and he noticed that he had everyone's attention.

"What we have here is a very ugly legal case. Do we uphold our non-interference directive and return these people back to their homes? Or do we not make a report of this find because of the volumes of archaeologists that would follow out here to answer the seven-century-old riddle. What happened to these people?"

"Captain, he's absolutely right, we simply cannot interfere with their cultures, however, we also must make a report of this find and henceforth all those who will come to study them. What do we do, sir?" asked the XO.

"The first thing is, we need the computer to speak their language. Find out, Personnel Officer, if anyone aboard can speak any of these languages. If there is no one to speak these languages, then, Computer Officer, modify the ship's computer's language bank to do its best job," said the captain.

"Yes, sir. I will do my best," he said, leaving the room.

"Now, we need to return those space people to their planet. Warrant Officer Weatherspoon, since you have some sort of possible rapport with these people, find out what you can as to how they came to be on the planet that they are on right now," said John.

"Yes, sir, I will do my best," replied Mike.

"I will contact STARCORE and inform them of this unique situation and see what they say we should do about it," said John.

With the meeting over, Mike went back down to the sickbay. Upon entering, he went straight to the holding cells and the young man stood up and bowed to Mike, as did the others. Mike returned the bow and the young man stepped forward towards Mike asking questions. Mike turned to the sickbay attendant and had her turn on the computer's linguistics bank. The computer listened to and then started translating the language as best it could.

"Are you a judge?" asked the young man.

"Of sorts. I do perform such limited judicial functions while aboard this starship," replied Mike.

Mike managed to get a good story from them all. He found out that they were the Mayans that mysteriously disappeared from Earth many centuries ago. They were all afraid that their abductors had returned to move them somewhere else during the middle of the night. Mike thanked them for their time and went straight to the captain's quarters.

"Yes, Warrant Officer Weatherspoon, what can I do for you?" asked John.

"I hope that you have a moment to discuss a potentially ugly legal issue, sir," said Mike.

"What kind of ugly legal issue?"

"I found out during my visit with our guests that they are the Mayans and that they were taken in the middle of the night to be placed on this planet. Sir, that amounts to forced relocation, now what do we do?"

"In other words, do we take the entire population back to Earth and let them live out their lives naturally in Central and South America or do we allow thousands of scholars to come here and possibly cause problems. You raise an interesting legal issue."

"Please present this information to STARCORE and ask them what we should do about this issue. By the way, I was right about that one structure, it is a prison of sorts and they have some sort of bicameral legislating body, one ruler of the people and a criminal justice system."

"Is that how that young man identified you?"

"Yes, sir. It would appear that their criminal justice system has parts of both an adversarial and inquisitorial system together. If this is true, then several dozen law books will have to be rewritten,"

"Why?"

"An inquisitorial and adversarial system cannot coexist."

"I see what you mean. If you find out any more details, be sure to let me know. I will advise STARCORE on this new development; dismissed," said John.

"Yes, sir."

Mike went to bed that night.

CHAPTER 10

Mike woke up early the next morning. He put on the uniform of the day and attached his rank to the left side of the tunic and his balanced scales with the quill across them on the right side. He went up to the wardroom to have breakfast and noticed that the whole place was buzzing with excitement. After finishing off breakfast, he went down to his office. He walked into his part of the office and looked around to find his coffee cup and decided to get a cup of coffee. As he walked out of the office, he stopped to look at LA2 Groder.

"Mr. Groder, what is on the agenda for today?" asked Mike.

"Three write-ups headed for Captain's Mast, sir," he replied.

"Please have them assemble in my office in half an hour, with their paperwork and we will see what we can do," said Mike, going to get his cup of coffee.

"Yes, sir," replied LA2 Groder.

Mike returned a few minutes later and sat down in his office. He looked over the Captain's Mast cases and had LA3 Monks and LN3 Bjork both sitting in on the cases. The first case to show up to his office was an engineer. He stood in front of Chief Warrant Officer Number One Mike Weatherspoon and saluted. Mike returned his salute.

"At ease," said Mike.

The man relaxed his attention stance. He didn't say anything while Mike looked over his case. Mike found some odd things in the write-up from the Chief Engineer on the issue.

"Do you know what you are being charged with?" asked Mike.

"Yes, sir, I am being charged with violating the STARCORE Uniform Code of Military Justice, Article 99, sir," he said.

"How do you plead?" asked Mike.

"Guilty, sir," he replied.

"Why do you think you're guilty?"

"I must not have performed the maintenance check correctly, sir," he said.

"Okay, Miss Monks?" he said turning towards her.

"Yes, sir?" she asked.

"Get me a copy of the Preventative Maintenance System Check-Card that this person was supposed to do and get it back to me soon," said Mike.

"Yes, sir," she said, leaving the room.

"Okay, so you think you violated the PMS check. Who wrote you up?" asked Mike,

"My division officer, the Damage Control Assistant and the Chief Engineer, sir,"

"Why did they write you up?"

"They did a spot check on my PMS check. Apparently, there were several steps that I missed that I don't think were on the PMS card, sir," he replied.

"Warrant Officer Weatherspoon, I have a copy of that PMS Check-Card, that you requested, sir," said Miss Monks, entering the room.

"Thank you, standby," said Mike.

Mike reviewed the PMS Check-Card and discovered several things that were in the man's favor. The first thing that Mike discovered was the date on the card was 1 January 2113. He looked down the card and then discovered that there were several things that should be done that weren't written on the card in the instructions phase. Mike looked up at the man.

"How many times has this PMS check been performed?" asked Mike.

"I was the first one to perform that particular PMS check, sir," replied the man.

"No one else had performed this check before you?" asked Mike.

"No, sir, no one else. This was a brand new PMS check on that piece of damage control equipment," he replied.

"Well, I have no further questions for you, right now. I will see you at Captain's Mast, dismissed," said Mike returning the man's salute.

"Yes, sir," he replied after the salute was completed.

Once the man had left the office, Mike handed the person's record over to Mr. Bjork. Mr. Bjork put the man's record into the computer terminal and looked over at Mike. Mike took in a deep breath and let it out slowly.

"I am ready to type in your comments, sir," he said.

"Upon discovering that this PMS check has never been done by anyone on this particular piece of damage control equipment and the fact that this PMS Check-Card is missing certain steps in the instructions block of the performance of the required maintenance check, I recommend 90 days suspended sentence," said Mike.

"Anything else, sir?"

"Recommend that the PMS Check-Card be updated to include these missing steps in the instructions block so that this problem will be prevented from occurring in the future," said Mike.

"Yes, sir."

The man's case was sealed up with Mike's electronic signature. Miss Monks informed Mike that the next case was waiting in the outer office. He asked her to bring in his case. He looked at the charge, "Possession with intent to sell/distribute a Schedule III, Level 2, Controlled Substance." Mike looked at the case and then asked for the person to be lead into the office. Miss Monks returned with the smallest humanoid that Mike had ever seen. The man saluted and Mike returned the salute. In Mike's eyes, the person was nothing more than a skeleton with a uniform on the outside.

"You are being charged with Possession with the intent to sell/distribute a Schedule III, Level 2, Controlled Substance, how do you plead?" asked Mike.

"Guilty of the possession part but I had no intent to distribute what drug I had, sir," said the man, looking down at the floor.

"According to this report, you had in your possession 30 autopen injectors of this controlled substance. That right there is enough to land you in a military prison for five years and a dishonorable discharge, coupled with a criminal record that will follow you for the rest of your life," said Mike.

"I know, sir, but the risk was worth it as far as I'm concerned, sir," said the man, looking up at Mike.

"At ease, what department do you work in?" asked Mike.

"Security, sir," the man replied with tears starting to show in his eyes.

"Relax, son. Where were these 30 autopen injectors that were supposedly in your possession?" asked Mike.

"In my private locker in my quarters, sir. I had ordered them from a black-market supplier and received them at the last port of call the ship made."

"You purchased something through the black-market? How do you know what you purchased is even the real thing?" asked Mike.

"I purchased the items from a STARCORE Medical Clearinghouse on Beta Cassini IX, sir. I have no doubt that the items are real, sir," he replied.

"Miss Monks, where are these 30 autopen injectors?" asked Mike.

"Evidence storage lock-up, Deck BB, Bin 290, sir," she replied.

"How tall are you?" asked Mike.

"1.3 meters, sir," the man replied.

"How much do you weigh?"

"50 kilograms, sir."

"How old are you?"

"26, sir."

"Let me talk to the Security Officer before I make any other plans for your defense. Right now, I must advise you of your rights, which I see have already been read to you when you were taken into custody."

"I am aware of my rights, sir."

"You do have several options at this point. Option A, general court-martial. Option B, Military Tribunal. Option C, plead guilty and spend the next five years of your life at the military penal colony of Antilles 2, receive a dishonorable discharge and lose everything. What is your plea?"

"Military tribunal, sir."

"So noted. Miss Monks, please schedule a military tribunal in accordance with STARCORE instructions," said Mike.

"Yes, sir," she replied leaving the office.

"Have you chosen your legal defense person, yet?"

"No, sir. I figured I would stand tall and answer for my crime, sir. However, am I allowed to have legal counsel at this military tribunal?"

"By STARCORE regulations, yes."

"I choose Mr. Bjork, sir. I trust him as much as I trust you, sir."

"So noted, dismissed," said Mike, saluting the man.

"Yes, sir," the man replied, returning the salute.

The man walked out of the office and the last case was brought into the office. The person, a female, was written up for having sexual relations inside of the ship's armory while on duty. She entered the office and Mike looked up at her. She saluted and he returned her salute.

"At ease," said Mike.

"Yes, sir," she said.

Mike was reviewing the in-deck flight recorder of the ship's armory. The snippet showed the young woman and a young man having sex. By the time the act was completed, Mike, Mr. Fracks, and Miss Monks were convinced that the female was guilty. However, Mike had other thoughts. He looked up at the female and noticed her facial features indicated she was from the Hanoid System.

"Are you Catian, by any chance?" asked Mike.

"Yes, sir," she replied, with a slight hiss this time.

"Recommend 90 day suspended sentence due to the female being a Catian. Her being a Catian and possessing certain unusual sexual proclivities resulted in the young male carrying on sexual relations with her while they were both on duty in the ship's armory. Further recommend that this female be advised to wait to have sexual relations with males until both are off-duty and advise males of the unique sexual characteristics of Catian females," said Mike.

Miss Monks typed up the recommendations and had Mike electronically sign the recommendations part of the write-up. The form then went into the computer and up to the captain for review. Mike dismissed the female and waited until the door had shut before speaking.

"It is almost lunchtime. Everyone go have something to eat and meet back here after lunch," said Mike.

"Sir, I'm a little nervous about being that young man's defense attorney. As you know, I have lost some cases and I have won others."

"What are you trying to say, Counsel Man Bjork?" asked Mike.

"Respectfully request your guidance on this case, sir," he replied.

"We will discuss tactics after lunch, Counsel Man Bjork," Mike replied, seeing a warm glow come to Mr. Bjork's cheeks.

While Mike was up in the wardroom, he noticed that both Captain Powers and Captain Laguer were nowhere to be seen. He looked around and noticed that the Medical Officer and the ship's Communications Officer were also missing from the regular lunchtime crowd. As he was getting ready to leave, Captain Powers entered into the wardroom. He came over and stood in front of Mike.

"We need to talk, Mike. STARCORE has issued instructions for us and they involve you," said John.

"Aye, sir. Where do you wish to discuss this issue, sir?" asked Mike.

"My underway cabin on the bridge in 20 minutes. By the way, what happened to those captain's mast cases I sent to you?"

"I have put my recommendations into the recommendations area for your review on two of them. There is one that has requested a military tribunal, sir," said Mike.

"A military tribunal? That must be done in 20 days, right?" asked John.

"Yes, sir. But that 20 days assumes that the vessel is within STARCORE space and that there are other STARCORE vessels within that 20 day range to hold the tribunal aboard, sir."

"Are you trying to get a continuance on the case?" asked John.

"Who says that I am representing him, sir?" asked Mike in return.

"I assumed you would be representing a member of the crew in a situation like this, Mike," said John.

"I offered my services, sir, however, the accused declined my services and, instead, requested Counsel Man Bjork, sir."

"Very well, make sure that you are in my underway cabin within the hour," said John.

"I will be there, sir," said Mike, standing up and taking his tray over to the scullery line.

Mike returned to the office and found that he had a little bit of time left before he had to report to the captain's underway cabin for a briefing. Counsel Man Bjork entered Mike's office and closed the door behind him. He handed Mike an electronic Letter of Withdrawal as Counsel for the Accused. Mike reviewed it and then handed it back to Counsel Man Bjork.

"Denied, Counsel Man Bjork," said Mike, electronically signing the form and handing it back to LN3 Bjork.

"What?! Why!?" he asked.

"The accused specifically requested you, not me."

"I don't think that I am ready for a military tribunal, yet, sir," he said pleadingly.

"Well, I told you that I would help your case out as best I could and I am going to do just that. However, I have a meeting with the captain in his underway cabin in a few minutes. When I get back, please have ready your defense packet and I will review it."

"Yes, sir."

Mike left and went to the captain's underway cabin. He knocked on the door and then entered. After saluting the captain, he remained at attention. Captain Powers looked up at him and smiled.

"Relax, Warrant Officer Weatherspoon. I need to inform you of STARCORE's decisions about our guests and how STARCORE personnel are to handle themselves around these people, among other items," said John.

"Yes, sir. I am ready to discuss any suggestions that either you or STARCORE has come up with on this current situation, sir," said Mike.

"STARCORE believes that what we have done out here is playing with a double-edged sword and it will cut both ways. Do you understand me, so far?" asked John.

"Yes, sir, I do understand you, sir," said Mike, making mental notes in his head.

"STARCORE wants me to return our guests to their people. After that is accomplished, STARCORE wants you to draw up legal documents that will dictate how STARCORE deals with these various peoples."

"In other words I am now a diplomat, sir? I have no formal training, sir," said Mike.

"Yes. STARCORE wants you to be their ambassador of good will and work something out with them."

"You mean, as to how STARCORE can meet with these people, sir?"

"Yes. STARCORE cannot get anyone else out here for several more months. STARCORE wants you to deal with these people and work out something that will allow STARCORE's legal, medical, archeological and other personnel access to them for study purposes."

"Why me, sir?"

"I told STARCORE that you had some rapport with them. STARCORE felt that since you have this rapport with their people, you could work something out. As of now, you are no longer this ship's legal officer, you are now an ambassador. You will travel to the planet's surface and report to me, every six hours, on your progress. Failure to report at the six hour mark will result in me sending down an armed landing party."

"I understand, sir."

"You are to report to the hangar deck as soon as possible to join our guests."

"Yes, sir."

"Dismissed," said John.

Mike left the captain's underway cabin. He returned to the office to find Counsel Man Bjork standing in Mike's office doorway holding his electronic clipboard. Mike walked inside the office and motioned Bjork inside the office. After the door was shut, Mike sat down in his chair and started reviewing what Bjork had written down. Mike only found a few things that Bjork had missed.

"Make sure that before each day of the tribunal that your uniform is pressed and clean," said Mike, as he handed back the clipboard.

"Yes, sir," replied Bjork, making notes on his electronic recorder

"I might request for a copy of the accused's blood and tissue samples that were taken by STARCORE when he entered STARCORE Service."

"Yes, sir. That thought had not crossed my mind, sir," he said, writing the notes down.

"I would also recommend a testing of one of the autopens to see what is inside of the autopen. Have you prepared an opening statement?" asked Mike.

"Not yet, sir. I'm working on it, though."

"Okay. Well, I have turned into an ambassador by STARCORE to work out legal documents as to how these people want to be treated by STARCORE."

"You'll be gone then, sir?"

"Yes and I don't know how long. Do you know where the tribunal is going to be held, yet?"

"Yes, sir. The tribunal is to be convened aboard the USS CARL VINSON, sir. I am to take a long-range shuttlecraft to meet their long-range shuttlecraft."

"I wish you luck. Are any of this ship's personnel going with you?"

"Yes, sir. Six persons for transport, me, the shuttlecraft pilot and the witnesses against the accused, sir."

"Very well. Let me know what happens."

"I will, sir,"

"Do you have any idea why your client would take this high a risk?"

"Not yet. I figure that the shuttlecraft flight will give me the time to find that information out."

"I wish you luck," said Mike, saluting Counsel Man Bjork.

"The same to you, sir," replied Counsel Man Bjork, returning the salute.

"Attention, all hands, attention, all hands. Counsel Man Bjork and Chief Warrant Officer Number One Weatherspoon, report to hangar deck control," said the communications officer's voice.

Mike gathered up his portable computers and walked with Bjork to hangar deck control. An airman apprentice met them and escorted them to their respective shuttlecrafts. Both men looked at each other one last time and saluted each other. Mike then stepped aboard his shuttlecraft and Mr. Bjork aboard his. The shuttlecrafts departed at around the same time but turned away in different directions.

An hour later, Mike was standing with his newfound friends in a great, black marble hall. A full military guard escorted Mike to meet the ruler of this planet. When the great wooden doors closed behind him, Mike knew his battle was about to begin.

Meanwhile, Counsel Man Bjork was seated across from his client on the shuttlecraft. He looked at his client and then at the guards. Counsel Man Bjork cleared his throat.

"May I please have some privacy to confer with my client?" asked Counsel Man Bjork.

"Sure, we will walk to the back of the shuttlecraft. What a loser for a client," scoffed one of the security personnel.

Counsel Man Bjork waited until the security officers had left and were out of earshot. He then leaned over to face his client and to speak to him without too many ears overhearing the conversation.

"Why did one of those security officers call you a loser?" asked Counsel Man Bjork.

"I'm not very aggressive, sir. I'm only on the ship's security force because there was no other place that I could go to when I arrived onboard. If you look at the rest of the ship's security force, you will notice that they are big, strong and VERY aggressive."

"And I surmise that this non-aggressiveness is a little issue with your fellow crewmembers?" prodded Counsel Man Bjork.

"What exactly is your job within the ship's security force?"

"I graduated from STARCORE Master-At-Arms School. I was assigned to the USS PERFORMANCE and, here I am, before you, for possession with the intent to sell/distribute a Schedule III, Level 2, Controlled Substance," said the man, bowing his head down low as if in shame.

"Since I don't have the lab report back yet on what is in those autopens, can you tell me what is in those autopens?" asked Counsel Man Bjork.

"Male hormone,"

"Steroids? Why would you be willing to take a substance that has dangerous, if not deadly, side effects?"

"I figured that since both the STARCORE Process Entry Facility and the ship's Medical Officer missed the fact that my testicles don't produce enough or even any male hormone, I wouldn't be able to get a legal prescription for the male hormone."

"So, you ordered the controlled substance from a STARCORE Medical Clearinghouse facility. Did you use any of those autopens?"

"No, sir. I tried at least half a dozen times to inject myself with them, but I couldn't bring myself to do the act."

"I don't think I could either. Now, try to get some rest while I work on your defense," replied Counsel Man Bjork as he waved his left hand at the security detail.

"Yes, Counsel Man Bjork?" asked one of them.

"My client is tired and would like to go to sleep,"

"If he will follow me," said the man.

A few hours later, Counsel Man Bjork and the accused were transferred to another long-range shuttlecraft. A few hours after that, Counsel Man Bjork and the accused were being welcomed aboard the USS CARL VINSON. The accused was taken to their ship's brig and Counsel Man Bjork was shown to his quarters. Counsel Man Bjork knew that the tribunal would convene the next morning. He put his head down on the pillow and went to sleep, dreaming of what Mike was possibly doing on the surface of the planet that was so far behind him now.

CHAPTER 11

Mike was completing up some reports when, suddenly, he could hear shouting, shooting and explosions. Mike walked over to the door and opened it just a crack. He peered down the hallway towards the ruler's chambers and saw the ruler's executive security personnel fighting with some people.

There was more shouting and suddenly the group divided and headed towards Mike's room. Mike shut the door and moved several pieces of heavy furniture in front of the door. He opened the window to his room and saw lots of military or paramilitary personnel all over the place.

He could also see military vehicles and, suddenly, the area he was in was bombarded by what Mike had been taught at STARCORE as being mortars. Missiles and rockets followed these mortar rounds; explosions were occurring all over the place.

Mike grabbed his transmitter and recorded a quick message; he hit the green button on the side of the transmitter, which would delay the transmission by one minute. He set the transmitter down and waited as more rockets and mortars came into the city.

The door was starting to give way. Constant pounding from the outside had moved the heavy pieces of furniture. With a few more pounds, the door was turned into splinters by an explosion. Mike immediately ducked down to the floor and covered his head to prevent from being hit with shrapnel.

Mike looked up and saw some people who grabbed him and then grabbed his equipment. They roughly handled him towards the door and strong-armed him to one of their military vehicles. He looked around at the dead bodies of his Mayan escorts and of the scenes around the palace. Blood and bodies were everywhere.

Mike was tossed into this vehicle and it quickly sped out of the city. Mike realized that he was a hostage. His only hope, now, was that the transmitter had not been damaged and would transmit, to the ship, his prerecorded message.

Suddenly, the lights went out for Mike as one of the people, who was holding him down, put a bag or cloth over his head. Mike did what he had been taught to do at STARCORE, do not resist. Resistance, although Mike was sure that he could handle them, would only serve to heighten their anger. Mike was down on the floorboard of the military vehicle he was riding inside. The vehicle came to a stop and Mike was strong-armed once again out of the vehicle and tossed by several people into a small room.

Once Mike was sure that there was no one in the small room he was inside of, he noticed that his hands had not been bound. After he stood up, he removed the cloth bag that had been put over his head. He looked around the small room and determined that he was inside of a cell of some kind. He carefully inspected the walls, the door and the window.

The door to the cell opened a short time later and his equipment was put inside with him. He noticed that the equipment had not been damaged and when the door had shut once again, he turned the equipment on. Now, at least he had a way to possibly communicate with the ship if the need were to arise. As he went about conducting his business, as if nothing had happened, the door opening interrupted him.

The person standing at the door pointed his automatic weapon at Mike and motioned Mike, using the muzzle of the automatic weapon, to follow him out of the door. Mike nodded his head up and down, stood up and walked out of the cell he was occupying. After stepping from the cell, the man used the muzzle once again to signal Mike to walk down a hallway.

When the man and Mike arrived at the end of the hallway, the man pointed his right index finger, this time at Mike and then at the doorknob. Mike opened the door and walked into a large arena of sorts. Mike estimated that the structure was more than 150 meters long, 200 meters wide and 400 meters tall. In the center of this arena was a large bomb of the likes Mike had only seen in history books. The man pointed at the bomb and shouted at the top of his lungs at Mike.

"USAF! USAF!" the man shouted.

"Yes, sir," said Mike as he started walking towards the missile.

Mike arrived at the bomb and looked it over carefully. He could see why the man was yelling USAF at Mike. There, on the side of the bomb, were the letters U.S.A.F.

Mike rolled his eyes and said, "United States Air Force."

The man nodded his head and then lowered his weapon. He put the weapon over his left shoulder as another man entered the arena. The man walked right up to Mike and smiled.

"Yes, you're quite right. This bomb belongs to the United States Air Force on planet Earth, North American continent," said the man in plain English.

"Sir, do you know what year it is on Earth?" asked Mike.

"Sure, it is sometime in October of 1960," the man replied.

"Oh, dear, sir. It is now the year 2113 on Earth. You are on another planet other than earth, sir. Do you know how you got here?" asked Mike.

"No. All I remember was flying in the bomb bay of my B-52 Stratofortress when there was a really bright light and I woke up here. You say the year is 2113 on Earth?"

"Yes, sir, it is."

"Then, who are you?"

"I'm Chief Warrant Officer Number One Mike Weatherspoon, Legal Officer, USS PERFORMANCE, NCX-2105, STARCORE, sir. Why did your men kidnap me, sir?" said Mike.

"I remember being told by the people on this planet that if more visitors came after they left, I was to set this bomb off and kill everyone I could. I had my men kidnap you so you could be at what we used to call ground zero," replied the man.

"Then this bomb is a thermonuclear type device?"

"Yes, on earth it was called a 100 megaton Hydrogen bomb. However, this one is unique. This bomb has a four-inch thick Plutonium ring around the payload. When the bomb goes off, the Plutonium gets vaporized and radiation levels on this planet will be high for many millennia to come," said the man, smiling.

Mike looked over the man who was starting to laugh. Mike looked back at the bomb. There, on the nosepiece, something was missing. Mike looked at the nosepiece once again. There was a small hole in the front.

"I'm just carrying out my orders, you do understand that, right?" said the man, who was now swinging around an odd looking pin attached to a ring.

Mike ran up to the man and grabbed the key from him. Mike turned the key over. The faded orange tag that was attached to it read, "REMOVE PIN TO ARM DEVICE." Mike closed his eyes and gave the man back the key.

"You do realize that everyone will die from radiation poisoning when this bomb goes off, right?" said Mike, smiling.

"Yes, that is why the timer was set to 10 minutes. It's been eight minutes now. We don't have long to wait," said the man, smiling.

"Well, you're right about that."

A few seconds later, Mike could faintly hear laser weapons fire coming from outside the door. He ran over to the door to the arena and saw the Mayan military moving in to rescue Mike. Mike was pounding on the glass windows in the hallway trying, with a futile attempt, to get their attention. Mike then ran back into the arena. The man was looking at his watch.

"How long has it been?" asked Mike.

"Nine minutes, ten seconds according to my bombardier watch," said the man, putting the old pocket watch back into his right front pocket of the jacket he was wearing.

More laser pistol and automatic weapons fire was heard. Suddenly, the whole place where Mike was standing inside of came under heavy weapons fire. Missiles, rockets and mortars were coming in at a record pace. Mike couldn't determine when one explosion had stopped and another started. He turned around to the man.

"How long has it been?" asked Mike.

"Nine minutes, forty-four seconds," replied the man as he lit up a cigarette.

Mike turned around as he saw men from the USS PERFORMANCE charging down the hallway towards him. As they came closer, he could see LN3 Bjork and LA1 Fracks in the lead. Behind them were MA1 Masterson and LN2 Groder. Everyone arrived and MA1 Masterson shot the man with a stun charge. He lead a group right straight down to the bomb and then had the group circle the arena checking for more people. Finding none, MA1 Masterson arrived back up to where Mike was standing.

"We are here, sir. It's time to go," said MA1 Masterson.

"I thought I made my message to the captain very clear," said Mike, a little frustrated that they had come to rescue him.

"You did. We decided that you were worth the pending court-martial for disobeying a lawful order from a superior officer. However, sir, you showed us that you are one of us and not a snob like other officers of STARCORE," said LN3 Bjork.

"Well, thank you. I truly appreciate what you did for me. However, do you see that object in the middle of the arena?" asked Mike, pointing at the bomb.

"Yes, sir. It is a bomb of some kind," said LA3 Monks.

"Yes, a thermonuclear bomb built on Earth called a Hydrogen bomb and it's set to go off any second now. Get a hold of the ship, have them send down someone to disarm this thing."

"Yes, sir," said LA1 Fracks.

"MA1 Masterson, take that man and put him in the ship's brig until I can straighten out this mess," ordered Mike.

"Yes, sir."

MA1 Masterson put handcuffs on the bombardier and then removed him. A few minutes later, Karl, from the ship's armory, showed up with various devices and a toolkit. He winked his right eye at Mike as he walked by heading towards the bomb. He set all of his equipment down in front of the bomb and started scanning it over carefully. After a few minutes, he smiled, took out an electric powered drill and attached a star nut driver head to the drill.

Mike turned around to see Karl smiling as he removed all 12 screws holding the front of the bomb together. He carefully removed the front plate and looked inside. He found the green and red wires going into and out of the barometer and cut the green wire. After this was done, he carefully removed the barometer and set it down on the floor. Next, he put on his entire radiation suit including the gloves for the next part.

Karl, still smiling, removed the Plutonium ring and set it off to the other side. He then went to remove the Plutonium triggering device and discovered that it didn't have one. The place where the trigger was supposed to be was empty. Removing his radiation suit, Karl stood up and gathered up his equipment. Karl started laughing even louder as he walked up to Mike and patted him on the back, tossing him the barometer.

"The bomb was a dud, sir," said Karl, walking off with all his equipment.

"A dud?" asked Mike.

"Yes, sir. The space where the Plutonium trigger was supposed to be was empty. The bomb is completely harmless and, if I am not mistaken, this bomb is now STARCORE museum property," said Karl.

"Yes, you're right, this bomb is museum property. Make sure someone collects this property up and it gets to its rightful owners," said Mike.

"Yes, sir," said LA1 Fracks.

Everyone returned to the ship. Karl was given a clean bill of health by ship's medical officer and all seemed well except for the bombardier. He was still in the ship's brig. After filling his report, Mike had a meeting with the captain in his underway cabin.

"I read your report and I want to tell you that STARCORE was extremely happy with your legal documents. I also want to tell you that your rescue party will not be charged," said Captain Powers.

"Thank you, sir. What about the bombardier, sir?" asked Mike.

"He will be returned to earth and allowed to live out his life naturally," replied John.

"Does he have any family?" asked Mike.

"I don't know."

"Please, sir, let me find out if he had any family and I will forward that up in a report."

"Very well. Could you please try to find out what happened to him?" asked John.

"Yes, sir."

Mike returned to the office. He stepped into the office and pointed at both Mr. Bjork and Miss Monks. They followed Mike into the office and Miss Monks shut the door. Mike made a nod of his head and she locked the door.

"Miss Monks, I need you to find out if that bombardier's story is true or not. I also need you to find out if he has any family members still alive," said Mike.

"Yes, sir," she replied, unlocking the door and leaving the office.

"Mr. Bjork, I read your report on the military tribunal. Good work, you made the military tribunal believe you and your client despite the evidence being presented against him. You have done well, I will recommend that you be allowed to attend STARCORE Legal Corps Academy on Earth at the next opportunity," said Mike.

"Thank you, sir," he said with a big smile on his face.

"Dismissed."

Mr. Bjork left the office. Mike went about looking over some of Mr. Bjork's cases that he had lost and some that he had won. Mike determined that all Mr. Bjork had to do was choose between those cases that he could defend and those cases that he could not defend. Mike closed the last case up that Mr. Bjork had worked on before he arrived. He put his recommendations into the report and re-filed the cases. Mike had just closed the drawer when he heard a knock on the office door.

"Enter," said Mike.

Miss Monks entered carrying her electronic clipboard. She closed the door and waited for Mike to sit down at his desk. She stood up at attention and looked down at her clipboard.

"What did you find out, Miss Monks?" asked Mike.

"In reference to the question about the bombardier having any living relatives on Earth, I did find one relative, sir," she said.

"Good, I will let the bombardier know that he at least has someone to go home to; a male or female relative?" asked Mike.

"A male relative, sir," she replied.

"Good. Make sure to send an advanced announcement through appropriate STARCORE channels about this pending arrival," said Mike, taking some notes on his personal electronic note recorder.

"I will take care of that, sir."

"What about the bombardier's story? Did it check out?" asked Mike.

"Yes, sir, the story did check out, sir."

"Would you please brief me?" asked Mike.

"Yes, sir. According to STARCORE archive records, a lone B-52 Stratofortress left a United States Air Force airbase just outside of what was known as Amarillo, Texas," she started off.

"What year was that?"

"The date was April 14, 1959. The plane, designated by the United States Air Force as Flight 29, took off at 0606 hours Central Standard Time. At or about 1009 hours, Flight 29 disappeared into a heavy fog bank. This was approximately four hours into her flight."

"Well, it sounds as if we have solved another mystery. Please continue."

"While flying in this heavy fog bank, Flight 29 disappeared off of the RADAR scopes of what was then known on Earth as the North American Aerospace Defense Command."

"I remember reading about that facility, it was very advanced for its time," commented Mike.

"An intensive air and ground search turned up nothing. The United States Air Force officially called off the search on May 1,

1959. Here's where the official report ends and speculation begins as to what happened."

"Does the United States Air Force records show how many people were aboard that plane?" asked Mike.

"Yes, sir. According to the United States Air Force there were four people aboard Flight 29. There was a pilot, a copilot, a navigator and the bombardier."

"What happened to the others?"

"According to records, since no wreckage of Flight 29 ever was found, it was surmised that the plane self-destructed in midair."

"Do the United States Air Force records show what was aboard Flight 29?"

"Yes, sir. A single, fusion type bomb. Officially classified as a Hydrogen bomb, 100-megatons in size."

"Where was Flight 29 headed for?"

"A nuclear weapons testing ground in the State of New Mexico called White Sands, New Mexico according to the report."

"If my history serves me correctly, not too far from there is a town called Alamogordo, New Mexico, where the first atomic bomb was detonated. Sorry, please continue."

"This Hydrogen bomb was to be dropped on a makeshift 'city' as the report called it to see the effects of a blast from a bomb of that size. The detonation altitude was approximately 1,166 meters above the ground."

"Then why did the plane take off with a useless bomb aboard?" asked Mike.

"The report is not specific, but since there was no wreckage found of the plane, to include this thermonuclear device, the case was left open as a missing plane."

"Miss Monks, make sure that this case is labeled as closed. List only one survivor of Flight 29 in the file."

"Yes, sir. Is there anything else, sir?"

"Yes. Recommend that this bombardier receive all awards that he is eligible for from both the United States Air Force and STARCORE," stated Mike.

"Yes, sir."

"Also recommend family reintroduction for the bombardier."

"Yes, sir. Is there anything else?"

"Yes, on this case of finding the Mayans. Recommend to STARCORE that the brave men and women who served as my escorts while on the planet's surface receive STARCORE's highest commendation."

"Yes, sir," she said, writing down what he had just said.

"Since it's about dinnertime, why don't you complete this all up tomorrow and I will walk you out the door," said Mike.

Mike walked her out the door and was locking the door up, when Miss Monks turned to face Mike. Mike looked at her and cocked his head to the right a little.

"You want those Mayans that were escorting you to receive a commendation without being true STARCORE citizens, sir," she said.

"A mere paperwork formality, Miss Monks. Those people gave their lives to protect STARCORE and me. I figured that this is the best way to reward them for their gallantry. Have a good night, Miss Monks and I will see you in the morning," said Mike.

"I understand, sir."

Miss Monks departed company with Mike on Deck 29. She went and ate dinner in silence in the mess hall. Mike went to the wardroom and ate dinner with the rest of the officers in silence as well. After dinner he went to the ship's brig and talked to the bombardier.

"In the morning, sir, you will be informed that you have a relative with whom you can meet with when you return to Earth," said Mike.

"Thank you, sir. I didn't realize how much of a fool I was, until now."

"Considering the circumstances, I would have carried out my orders as well. Flight 29, which is the one you were on when it disappeared off the RADAR scopes at approximately 1009 hours Central Standard Time on April 14,1959, has but you as the survivor, sir."

"I buried the pilot, the co-pilot a few years later and the navigator a few years after that. All of them had died from radiation poisoning. The bomb had not been properly cleaned and radiation was leaking from it continuously."

"Were you checked over by our medical staff?"

"Yes, sir and I am alright for right now. I just appear to have a whole lot of catching up to do, when I get back to Earth."

"Would you like a tour of the ship?"

"Yes, sir I would like that very much."

"I will make the arrangements, then. I will be returning shortly."

"Thank you, sir."

"You're welcome and thanks for helping us solve two mysteries on this mission."

Mike left the brig and went to his own quarters. He undressed, showered and went to bed only to find Karl already asleep in his bed. Mike crawled into bed with him and drifted off to sleep.